ME

Augie sat dow... ...learly had something

"Can I get you a water? Coffee or tea."

"I'm fine thanks. But I have some news that I know you're not going to like."

"Is it about Rico and Isabella? You can't possibly think that you can build a case around a dough hook."

"It's not that."

"Then what? Spit it out, Augie."

"I had a meeting with Inspector Mason and his team this morning. They have determined that the fire's point of origin was in the attic that is open all the way through the mall. Some of the proprietors used it for extra storage. The fire was started above the drugstore."

"Okay, that should completely exonerate the Brunos. I can't imagine them crawling over six stores' worth of stuff just to point the blame elsewhere. And they'd have to crawl all the way back before the fire got to them. They are innocent."

"For now, maybe."

"And?"

"Mason's team found thick glass shards where the fire started and were able to piece enough of them together to determine that a so-called Molotov cocktail was used as the incendiary device. There was a label on this bottle—it was a wine bottle. They found enough to be able to decipher the name. It was a claret and it was from the Abigail Rose Winery."

Books by Christine E. Blum

FULL BODIED MURDER

MURDER MOST FERMENTED

THE NAME OF THE ROSE

CLARETS OF FIRE

Published by Kensington Publishing Corporation

Clarets of Fire

A Rose Avenue Wine Club Mystery

CHRISTINE E. BLUM

KENSINGTON PUBLISHING CORP.

www.kensingtonbooks.com

KENSINGTON BOOKS are published by

Kensington Publishing Corp.
119 West 40th Street
New York, NY 10018

All Kensington titles, imprints, and distributed lines are available at special quantity discounts for bulk purchases for sales promotions, premiums, fund-raising, educational, or institutional use. Special book excerpts or customized printings can also be created to fit specific needs. For details, write or phone the office of the Kensington sales manager: Kensington Publishing Corp., 119 West 40th Street, New York, NY 10018, attn: Sales Department; phone 1-800-221-2647.

KENSINGTON BOOKS and the K logo are Reg. U.S. Pat. & TM Off.

First printing: October 2019

10 9 8 7 6 5 4 3 2 1

ISBN-13: 978-1-4967-2482-3
ISBN-10: 1-4967-2482-8

Printed in the United States of America

Electronic edition:

ISBN-13: 978-1-4967-2483-0 (e-book)
ISBN-10: 1-4967-2483-6 (e-book)

For first responders everywhere.

ACKNOWLEDGMENTS

A big thank-you to Fire Station 62 and to Captain Darin Laier, not just for providing background for my book but for protecting us in times of emergency. There wouldn't be a story if it weren't for the real members of the Rose Avenue Wine Club—I love you all. And Bardot, you barely lifted a paw in the writing of this book, but that won't stop me from giving you an extra biscuit.

Chapter One

"Welcome to the annual Rose Avenue block party," Peggy announced in her best outside voice while hoisting a brimming glass of Tooth & Nail cabernet.

"Hear, hear," replied several neighbors.

From the back corner of her yard, I canvassed the somewhat motley crew gathered on this beautiful, sunny September Sunday. I started with my inner circle of imbibers, dear friends that share the group moniker of the Rose Avenue Wine Club. They are listeners, sisters, partners in crime (literally), and the best friends a transplant from New York City could have. Since I moved to the sleepy, beach community of Mar Vista, California, nearly four years ago, I really haven't had a moment to look back. I'd wanted a new life and, boy, did I get it. It appears that in addition to us girls declaring wine tasting an Olympic sport, we also share a penchant for solving crimes and giving the perpetrators their proper due. Somewhat to the chagrin of the denizens of Rose Avenue but ultimately welcomed by them, unless of course, one of them committed the evil deed (which has happened once . . . or twice) . . .

From my vantage point, like a mobster in a restaurant facing the door with his back to the wall, I could see any new arrivals to the party. Peggy's yard, like her house, was kept pristine—perfectly trimmed boxwood hedges and weedless narrow flowerbeds lined the perimeter. I'd been witness to her methods of motivating her gardener on multiple occasions, and let's just say that the shortest route to living a long life involves doing Peggy's bidding. This octogenarian was showing no signs of slowing down.

Beside me sat my best-*est* friend, Bardot, the yellow Lab now famous for diving underwater and saving my life. I noticed that while she sat in a relaxed AKC conformation pose (she's a total ham), her nose was pointed skyward and her olfactory glands were pumping harder than the speakers at a Sir Mix-a-Lot concert. Unlike English Labs that would sell their soul for a morsel of anything even resembling food, Bardot is an American Field Lab and she is much more motivated by words like, "Ready? Go!" So I dismissed party snacks as the reason for her persistent pulsing proboscis, and that left me a little on edge and confused.

"Halsey! So happy that you and Bardot have saved me the best seat in the house," Sally shouted, making her way over to us while balancing a plate of fruit and cheese along with two filled wineglasses. I noticed that tucked under her arm was the accompanying bottle; I would expect nothing less from my closest Rose Avenue friend. I quickly jumped up to relieve her of the wineglasses but she held on tight, insisting instead that I take the plate. I watched as she lowered her lithe, African American frame down into a lawn chair while not spilling a drop of the grape elixir. I'd also managed to abscond with a small patio table, so we had room for all the food groups: wine, cheese, and wine.

"If you build it—" I laughed, noticing rosy-cheeked Aimee and Peggy making their way over to us. They too didn't arrive empty-handed. Too bad that Aimee couldn't provide some of her sinful frozen yogurt from her shop, but it wouldn't travel well on a day like today.

I may have to pop by the Chill Out for dessert . . .

"No sign of Penelope and Malcolm yet?" my silver-haired, madras shorts–clad friend Peggy asked.

While technically Peggy was the only other single lady in the Wine Club, we were both now officially off the market. A widow for almost ten years, she recently reconnected with an old friend and work buddy of her late husband's. His name is Charlie and the two quickly became "an item" as Peggy quaintly put it. Qualified by "and he lives in another area code half the time, which is just the way I like it." Charlie resides in San Diego but is conveniently a small plane pilot and can shuttle up to the Santa Monica Airport whenever he wishes. We'll get to my guy in a minute.

"I talked to Penelope about twenty minutes ago," Aimee said with a smiling, flushed face. They're coming directly from the airport. Malcolm's second cousin Andrew picked them up. She didn't have much time to talk but said that the honeymoon was dreamy."

The thought of that made her complexion turn even redder, so she waved her hands frantically in front of her face to cool her cheeks down. Aimee's emotions were always just a millimeter below the surface waiting to jump out, a fact that us jaded cynics find so endearing.

"I still replay that day in my mind just before I go to sleep each night; that was a magical wedding." Sally closed her eyes. The artist in her was coming out. "They looked happier than clams at high tide."

While from upstate New York originally and a retired nurse, Sally somehow had acquired a lexicon of Southern sayings that frankly should have stayed in the bayou. I suspect that one summer she binge-watched *The Beverly Hillbillies* and *Petticoat Junction* during a critical, young imprint age.

"Here comes trouble," I warned, seeing Marisol approach with two plates piled high.

"Make room for the mayor of Rose Avenue," Peggy said, shuffling us around the chairs to free one up in front.

"What a coincidence, like where there's paper there's plastic, where there's a couple fighting in public there's a hushed crowd pretending not to listen, and where there's free food there's Marisol. Did they run out of samples at Costco?"

"You need to respect your elders while you still have time, Halsey. With the amount of wine you drink, you won't make it to Christmas. But there's good news . . . when you drop, your body will already be embalmed."

With that Marisol let out a cackle direct from her belly that was so hearty my friends couldn't help but join in.

Let me explain a little about this strange creature that happens to be my next-door neighbor. Though we cajole, tease, insult, and generally bicker about anything from my dog's name to her constant spying, deep down we have enormous respect and love for each other. Just don't ask either of us to admit it. Marisol is somewhere between eighty-four and one hundred, hard to say because she never ages, or, I suspect, sleeps. She may be afraid that if she does nod off, she'll have boarded the train to the dark side. She has an uncanny knack for knowing everything about everyone, even before they know it themselves. She's continually learning (one of the handful of things I admire about her) and is currently mastering an array of high-tech spy equipage. All of this is hidden behind a façade of a diminutive Latina woman, a tad frail-looking with a coiffure of jet black–dyed hair kept in place with little butterfly clips. She also seems to appear and disappear at the blink of an eye. But, as much as her prying, long, caramel-colored nose annoys me, we have developed some sort of symbiotic relationship that compels us to save each other's bacon if it comes down to that. (Mind you I'd probably give my life for one last bite of bacon anyway.)

"Where's Jack?" Marisol asked, biting into a pig-in-a-blanket with such ferocity that mustard went running for its life out of both corners of her mouth. "He finally come to his senses and realize that I'm the one on Rose Avenue he should be dating?"

As ridiculous as her statement was, Marisol knew how to push my buttons and I fought hard not to show it. Instead, I forced my mind to picture a beautiful boat adrift on a calm, deep blue sea as dolphins playfully followed along and watched with fascination as I opened up the urn and scattered Marisol's ashes. "He'll be along shortly. He ran a certification test in

the Santa Monica Mountains this morning and went
home to shower and change."

"Saving more souls—what's your excuse?"

Marisol was referring to Jack (my guy as you probably guessed), and his volunteer job as a search and
rescue K-9 team instructor for CARA.

"I'd work on saving your soul if you had one,
Marisol."

I kept my right hand over my left and pondered if
this was the right moment to give the Wine Club girls
my revelatory news.

A round of applause erupted across the yard and
neighbors got to their feet. I thought that maybe Jack
had arrived and spilled the beans, but when people
sat back down I saw Malcolm and Penelope entering
the yard hand in hand and glowing.

For the briefest of moments my heart took an express elevator down to my stomach as I thought about
marriage and its trials and tribulations. I'd had one
lousy one and, like eating a bad oyster, I never wanted
to relive that experience.

"There they are!" Sally shouted. "More chairs, Aimee,
we need more chairs. And who's that cute fellow with
Malcolm and Penelope?"

"I'm guessing Andrew," Aimee said, and then told
some kids that the pizza was coming any minute and
they better move up front to get some. "Kids sit too
much anyway," she offered as explanation as she
"borrowed" their roosts and added them to our circle.

Penelope spotted us, waved, and gave Malcolm a
peck on the cheek before heading over. He responded with a wink and a knowing smile. It took
Malcolm some time to get used to our coterie of imbibers, but now he regarded us as family. At least I

think he does. He and I went through a rough patch, but that story is a present for another Christmas. He looked uncommonly relaxed for someone I always thought of as shy and was sporting a café au lait tan, probably the first for this light-complexion, ginger-haired man.

"Darlings, I've missed you all terribly." Penelope made the rounds giving us each hugs and kisses. I reminded myself of the probable need to have her translate some of her typical British expressions.

"Red or white?" Peggy asked Penelope, hovering both bottles over an empty glass.

"Ooh, is that an Oregon pinot blanc? Yes, please!"

While Peggy obliged Penelope, Aimee bombarded Penelope with questions about the honeymoon in such rapid fire that she resorted to nodding "yes" or "no" to the majority of them.

"I bet that you're anxious to get back to your beautiful winery. Now comes the hard part . . . getting it fully operational," I remarked.

"Agreed, although Malcolm's second cousin Andrew"—she waved to the two men talking across the lawn—"has been such a dear. He's gotten so much done while we were off on holiday. I've been told to get the wine tasting room and small bites menu in order for the fall harvest. You must all come and stay overnight so that we can have our first Rose Avenue Wine Club sleepover!"

"Sounds like a blast. What will you do while we're sleeping?" I asked Marisol.

"She can perhaps sort out the strange things that I've witnessed happening there in the wee hours," Penelope suggested. "I'm still getting used to sharing this old winery with spirits, and not the alcoholic ones!"

"I can do that. I'll need to bring some equipment though." I could see Marisol start making a mental list.

Just then Bardot's nose once again jerked up to the sky, knocking over my wineglass in the process. As I reached to grab it my engagement ring caught the sun, sending out a blinding beacon of light.

"Halsey, what is that on your finger?" Aimee shrieked.

I guess that this carbon cat is out of the bag.

The rest of the girls joined in the screaming and flocked around me like I was bread in a piazza full of pigeons.

"I need to hear the full story. How long have you been hiding this from us?" Sally almost seemed incensed.

"Jack actually started to propose at your wedding, Penelope, but Augie arrived and blew that out of the water. Even unwittingly he makes my life miserable. Remind me again why you invited him?" I gave Penelope a pretend dirty look.

"It was Malcolm's idea really; they spent quite a bit of time together during that whole, horrible garden affair."

Augie is our local detective, and our paths crossed literally on the day that I arrived on Rose Avenue and happened into the wrong house for Wine Club. How was I supposed to know that there was a dead body in the backyard? Or that when digging in the garden plot the girls got me for my birthday, I'd find another body?

Augie really needs to start believing in coincidences.

"Pizza's here!" we heard someone yell.

"I'll go help Enrico and Isabella." Aimee took off like a shot. Being in the food service industry herself, she knows what hard work it is. Although every time I go into her frozen yogurt shop, Chill Out, she makes everything seem so effortless. She really struggled the first year while her boyfriend Tom was in med school, but she's got some amazing flavors and has added cakes and pastries to the mix. The shop is now a Mar Vista fixture.

As is our cherished Rico's Pizza, neighborhood purveyor of delicious Italian pies baked just about a mile from Rose Avenue. I watched the husband and wife team set out the delicious food and let the wafting aromas permeate my proboscis. Bardot once again had her head in the air, but hers was pointed in the opposite direction from the spicy, cheesy airstream. This bothered me.

"Here's my hubby and his cousin," Penelope announced as Malcolm and Andrew approached.

Marriage suited Malcolm and he'd gone from looking like a red-haired Harry Potter to someone closer in appearance to Eddie Redmayne. He introduced Andrew to the group.

"In addition to being invaluable in the fields, Andrew will be instrumental in marketing the Abigail Rose Winery to the public," Malcolm explained.

"Yes," Penelope chimed in. "And Andrew's just secured a joint venture with Rico's Pizza! They will be serving our wine and I'll be offering individual artisan pizzas in our Tasting Room."

We all applauded.

"I couldn't have done it without these wonderful folks," Andrew said, and beamed as Enrico and Isabella Bruno approached. This was my first chance to get a good look at Malcolm's second cousin, and though not so uncommon, Malcolm looked nothing like him. Andrew had shoulder-length, dark, wavy hair, about a three-days' growth on his face, and I got the hint of a six-pack under his tight T-shirt.

Me likey. What am I saying? I'm betrothed!

"It sure smells like you've outdone yourselves again." I turned to Enrico and Isabella. "And now you'll be serving wine? Good luck getting me to go home." I smiled.

"Not *just* wine, but some of the winery's precious, young clarets," the precious, young Andrew corrected me.

"You guys aren't leaving, are you?" Peggy asked the Brunos.

"Have a glass of wine at least," Sally implored.

"I'm afraid that we have to get back to the restaurant; this is a very busy time for us," Enrico replied with a slight bow.

Isabella followed suit, "Football season has started." She gave a knowing head nod to us.

Who says football is just a spectator sport? It takes work and finesse to eat pizza without burning the roof of your mouth.

"Bye, Isabella. I'll pop over in a bit to keep you company while you prepare for the dinner rush," I said distracted by Bardot who had started whimpering and was looking agitated.

"Bardot, what is it, honey?"

"Maybe she's tired of all this and wants to go home and take a nap," Aimee suggested.

"Have you met my dog? She would never leave a party early."

Bardot responded by shoving her nose into the palm of my hand persistently.

"She really wants to show me something." I reattached her leash. "I'd better find out what."

On cue she thrust her nose in the air again.

"Does anybody else smell smoke?" Sally asked.

We all took in lungfuls of air and hesitantly nodded. Except for Marisol who launched a police scanner app on her phone and listened to the dispatch calls.

Eight-fifty-two, what's your location?

We've just arrived on the scene; fire appears to have fully engulfed the roofs of all the businesses in the strip mall. Need backup to help divert traffic from Centinela and Palms.

"That's where Rico's Pizza is!" Peggy shouted loudly to be heard over the sounds of approaching sirens.

Chapter Two

I do my best to keep up with Bardot, who, thanks to Jack's CARA training, was in full rescue mode running low to the ground and sweeping her nose left and right. We'd sped past the rest of the Wine Club, leaving them in our wake doing a full-on run up the hill of Rose Avenue. The smoke smell was getting intense. What I saw when we reached the top stopped me dead in my tracks.

The street was a sea of red as fire trucks arrived and deployed first responders from every direction. Brown and orange billows of thick smoke were quickly erasing the blue sky in exchange for an eerie glow. A crowd had started to gather in front of the gas station across the street from the strip mall.

Is that really a smart place to be spectating? Do they not remember the gas station scene in Hitchcock's The Birds*?*

Bardot had been equally stunned by the scene but was now back to her mission of pulling me closer to the scene and then around to the back of the fiery stores. When she settled on Rico's Pizza, she launched into a ten-bark sequence, a CARA signal that she had found the target. My heart dropped to my feet as I wondered if Isabella was inside. But I heard my name called and spotted her and Rico watching with horror from the sidewalk. At that moment Bardot lunged toward the back door of the parlor and her leash slipped out of my hand. She disappeared through a wall of smoke.

"Bardot, NO!"

I had no choice but to go in after her. The firemen were all fighting the blaze from what looked like the origin point on the roof. I slid into the place on my belly, trying to stay as low as possible to the floor.

"Bardot? Come!"

Nothing. I heard an ax being driven into the ceiling above me as they worked on making an opening for ventilation. Once they cut through and let in the air, all hell is going to break loose as I recall from binge-watching *Chicago Fire*.

"BARDOT!"

I picked up the faint sound of shuffling over the noise from above and could swear that I heard a growl. I took off my T-shirt and wrapped it loosely around my nose and mouth before shimmying farther into the room. When a piece of the ceiling fell down on me and a ray of light was let in, I could make out something yellow coming toward me.

More light flooded in and I realized that I was looking at the business end of Bardot and that she was backing out while dragging something with her.

We had precious few seconds. I lunged up to her head and felt more than saw that she had the collar of a person's shirt in her jaws. I found the person's shoulders and then underarms and secured my hold.

"One, two, three!"

Bardot and I put our entire body weights into

pulling the person to the door. We were close, and with one more countdown we were able to back into the parking lot. Sally had arrived and she brought reinforcements.

Paramedics and firefighters rushed to carry us a safe distance away just before the oxygen from the vent in the roof gave the fire new life and flames licked out and up the exterior of the building. If we'd been a few seconds slower, we would have been toast. Literally.

"Bardot?" I asked in a panic before I was muzzled by an oxygen mask.

"She's getting help too, honey, but she looks like she'll be fine," Sally assured me.

For the first time I had a chance to look around and take in the scene. People in the work clothes of their various trades at the stricken mall looked on despondent and helpless as they watched their businesses turn to soot and ash. News vans were parked haphazardly along the side street and were dislodging reporters and photographers. The fire on the top of the mall was burning with intensity, releasing ebony smoke into the sky. But the venting had sent all the oxygen-seeking flames to the roof, and responders could now go into the stores and douse embers. I caught sight of Bardot and saw that she had a child's breathing mask attached to her snout and was breathing and wagging her tail in three-four time. When I looked at her yummy paramedic, I completely understood her happy mood. It was then that I noticed that I was topless except for my bra, a nice pink and gray number with tea roses at the base of the straps. But still, even in this chaotic scene I stood out—attracting way too much attention.

"Halsey? What the hell happened and why do I always find you in the middle of a crime scene?"

Augie. Of course.

At that moment the crowd that had been gathered around the body we'd pulled out of the parlor began to separate. Isabella and Enrico were among them. She was crying as he led her away. We exchanged a brief look of concern for each other and I nodded that I was okay. In the clearing I could just make out that the rescue victim was a guy, maybe twenty. When the ambulance driver pulled a sheet over him, I closed my eyes and tried to slow my breathing. The mask was no longer necessary. What I needed now was my cozy bed and time to grieve.

Bardot was delivered to me contained by a make-shift rope leash. We were both going to need a long shower, but she seemed content that she'd done her job today. I wished I could say that I'd done the same.

"I've got a lot of questions for you, Halsey—is she cleared to talk now?" Augie asked my wonderful EMT, and he nodded and gave me a secret wink.

"Ask away, Augie. If your plan is to deal me a good dressing down, then I've given you a head start." I smiled sweetly at the EMT and the approaching fire-fighters.

"Here's a jacket for you, Miss . . . ?"

"Halsey. You can just call me that." I smiled up at the man in the helmet and red suspenders.

"We will need a full name for the report, Halsey. I'm Fire Chief Adam Pasquale." His premature gray hair and chiseled, kind face was sending me to my happy place. Until I remembered why I was here.

"Chief, I saw them cover the man that we pulled

out of the building. Is he really gone?" My voice cracked at the finality of it.

"I'm afraid so, but you did everything that you could. And I'll save the lecture, but what you two did"—he looked at Bardot who gave him her Hallmark Christmas card pose—"was a terrible risk and one that you will never do again, correct?"

"Halsey!" Peggy screamed, running to me with Aimee and Marisol in tow.

"She's okay, they both are," Sally assured everyone.

"How'd you get here so fast, Sally? I know Halsey took the Bardot express, but what's your secret?"

"Peggy, you know that I speed-walk every morning, and in a day I average about ten thousand steps."

"I'm impressed," the chief complimented her, and then turned his attention to Augie. "And you, sir, are you part of this fascinating group?"

"Only when they break the law." He showed the chief his badge.

"Oh, Augie, you know you love us." That was the cue that Bardot needed to jump on him with her wet paws and beg for some loving. For some reason Bardot is a fan of Augie. I keep trying to explain to her the importance of making the right choices.

"Get off me," he yelled at her, but it was too late. His white shirt was already emblazoned with two perfect, sooty pawprints.

"Bardot, come stand with me, honey. You can lick my hands; they smell of pizza," Aimee coaxed her.

"Augie, you know how this fire started?" Mayor Marisol was on the case.

I watched Augie's face flush a crimson red from his neck to his forehead in the span of three seconds.

The firefighters took in the diminutive Rose Avenue menace and, I'm guessing, tried to figure out what kind of hold she had on Augie.

"Marisol—"

She gave Augie a death stare.

"Er, Auntie, I am only here to offer assistance to the firefighters. This is their scene and we should let them get back to work."

Marisol gave him the kind of blank stare that the kids in a *Peanuts* cartoon give their scolding teachers.

"Chief, the captain from ACTS has arrived with his team, and they are standing by for a briefing."

Another cute firefighter. I've got to find the fountain from whence these guys spring.

"I'll be right there, thanks. Halsey, I'm going to send someone over to take your statement and get all your information." The chief gave my shoulder a squeeze.

"Someone with ACTS?" Augie asked, still looking like a paw-printed fish out of water.

The chief nodded and gave us a salute and a smile.

Where do I go to volunteer?

"Augie, they're sending someone over with an ax?" Marisol was trying to wipe his shirt with her sweater, and even I was beginning to feel sorry for him.

"ACTS, Auntie. It's an acronym for Arson/Counter-Terrorism Section."

"Arson. Interesting." Peggy's mind was off to the races.

"There's a terrorist on the loose? Go catch him, Augie!" Marisol pointed in a random direction.

"I'm on it, Auntie, and Halsey, I'll talk to you later."

His voice trailed away as he worked to put as much distance as possible between himself and Marisol.

We'd moved to a makeshift command center in the parking lot with chairs and a table set up under a pop-up canopy. Bardot and I had been given water, and Sally had stayed with me for moral support. Heaven knows where Marisol was, probably dressing for combat. Enrico and Isabella were huddled in another corner of the shelter and were speaking with an investigator. I wanted to go over and hug Isabella tightly; she and Enrico had just lost their entire livelihood. One they worked so hard to establish. How do they pick up the pieces and rebuild?

"Hi, I'm Inspector Mason, and you are Halsey?" he assumed by the soot and loaner jacket that I was wearing.

"Yes, hi. This is my friend Sally, and the one with the fur pants is Bardot."

He didn't crack a smile. *Not a good sign.*

"Maybe Sally could take your dog home; they really don't need to be here."

I looked at Sally while his words hung in the air. Finally, I nodded.

"I'll be close by." Sally waved her cell phone at me.

"While you fill out some basic information on this form, I'm just going to take a couple photos of you for our records."

I looked at him in horror. I could only imagine what this frightening ordeal had done to my usually pleasant comportment.

He went to town with a camera app, and I could tell that this man knew nothing of proper photographic composition and lighting. As I went through the fields on the form—name, address, driver's license number, and so forth—I caught sight of the shadow of a person pacing on the other side of the canopy flap. Occasionally it would get real close, and the side turn of the head suggested that someone was trying to eavesdrop. I had a pretty good guess of who that "someone" could be.

I finished the last line and handed the sheet back to Inspector Mason. I was tired, hot, more than a little achy, and feeling a growing crank surface.

"Either go away or come inside; you keep standing out there you'll collapse from heat stroke. The paramedics have enough on their hands."

The inspector gave me a wide-eyed, stern look like I'd just become the host body for the devil. He turned to follow my stare, and slowly the flap parted and Augie entered the covered area.

"Who are you?" The inspector demanded.

Augie gave him his credentials.

"Halsey lives in my jurisdiction and we've had a few, let's say, encounters in the past."

"She has a record?" Mason asked.

"Augie, how dare you! Of course I don't have a record. This neighborhood detective seems to have trouble detecting crimes, and so he takes the easy route and blames me first. Ultimately, I have to point him in the right direction."

I knew that I was being a bit harsh in front of another serve and protector, but I'd had enough of today, and Augie's implication was just going to make the interrogation, as it now appeared to be, last longer.

"I won't interfere, Inspector, I'll just listen in.

Either way I have to take her statement, so why not do this once for both departments?"

Mason appeared to think about that for a minute. The canopy was now filled with ash particles in the air that emitted an acrid, caustic sweet smell. No one was happy to be here, and I was thankful that Sally and Bardot were not breathing this into their lungs. I coughed and felt a burning in my throat.

"The faster you clear up my questions, Ms. Hall, the faster this will be over." Mason had decided to ignore Augie, I guess.

He had me run through the sequence of events from the start of the block party until the present. He asked few questions but listened intently. He seemed to be focused on the timeline of my account. Ultimately, he drew it out on a piece of paper and had me estimate as close as possible the minutes at which each event occurred. My head was pounding and my crank had boiled into a full-on combustible temper. I noticed Isabella and Rico stand, and I waved them over.

"Are you guys okay?"

"As well as can be expected." Enrico looked shaky. "We are worried about you. What you did to try and save Roberto, it was, well, the kindness and bravery we have come to admire in you, Halsey."

"Roberto? That sweet guy who worked for you?" I asked, paying no attention to steam rising from Mason's head.

"He was our delivery driver," Isabella explained. "But we had no idea that he was in the building . . . his shift didn't start until five. So, so sad."

She resumed her weeping into Enrico's shoulder. She was about a foot taller than he was.

"They questioned you for quite a while, what was that all about? They can't possibly think that you had anything to do with this. You were with us delivering pizza to our party and visiting with friends." I joined Isabella for a group hug.

"That's what we explained, when we got back here everything was already in flames!"

"Enrico, calm down or you'll give yourself a heart attack." Isabella fixed his thick, dark hair from his eyes and fanned his face with her hand.

"Is that what this little drawing is about, Inspector? Are you trying to get me to say that they'd left the party before the fire broke out? Well my dog's nose says differently!"

"Hah!" Augie suddenly came to life.

"Enough. You two need to leave and let me finish my interview. I'm sure we'll contact you for a follow-up," Mason said to the Brunos, and waited until they'd left the tent.

"Now, let's resume," he said to me, turning his attention to the timeline again.

"No! I am done. You people have had me here for two hours in the heat and toxic air. And this is after I rescued a victim from a burning building, something that is your job. My throat is burning, and I can feel my lungs tightening. I could be facing a chronic breathing condition, and that will be on you, Inspector Mason."

I got up from the table.

As I pulled open the canopy flap, I heard Augie say, "We're going to need to question your dog's nose."

"You think this is funny, Augie? Someone died today."

"No, it's not funny." He looked contrite. I guess my reprimand had knocked some sense into him.

I turned back to leave and ran right into Marisol. *Now I understand Augie's change in demeanor.*

"Bardie's nose knows," she pronounced.

"What have I told you about calling Bardot by her full name?" I asked Marisol as we headed back to Rose Avenue.

"I dunno."

Chapter Three

As we reached our side-by-side houses, I saw Sally and Bardot perched on my front stoop talking to Jack.

"Halsey! Are you okay, babe?" he asked, scooping me up in his arms.

"Not really. That suspicious arson investigator kept me there for over an hour breathing in that toxic air."

"Arson? Wow, no wonder it took me forever to get here. Every street leading to Rose Avenue was blocked off, and I ended up leaving my truck at the Santa Monica Airport and jogged over here. How did you get involved with the fire? Sally wasn't entirely sure."

"I'm suffering from the smoke too." Marisol forced a gasping cough to punctuate the point.

"That's your own fault. You could have left at any time, but you just had to nose around."

"It just so happens that I am assisting with the investigation."

"On whose orders? Are you part of the volunteer fire department now, Marisol?"

"I could be."

"I'm just glad that you're both safe," said my amber-eyed redwood of a man as he gave me a kiss.

At a muscular six-foot-four, Jack could be an imposing figure to people, especially with his shaved head and close-cropped beard—but he has the kindest eyes that always have a twinkle and a heart to match his size. When he is not rescuing victims of accidents with his dog on behalf of CARA—Canine Rescue Association—he is saving pet owners by providing positive reinforcement dog training. In fact, that's how we met. I'd just moved here and was foolishly worried about Bardot falling in the pool and not knowing how to swim. She showed us. I sometimes suspect that she was playing matchmaker from the get-go. Jack makes his life about helping people with dogs. I wish that I could say I have an equally noble calling.

I make my living writing code and designing websites, and when I started my company in New York City during the tech bubble, I would never have imagined that I'd be plying my trade from a suburban house on a Chinese elm–lined street with a converted garage for an office. I have a small roster of steady clients like the Marina del Rey Coast Guard, but I could always use a few more. I am working on a site for the Abigail Rose Winery, but I would never charge them for payment in anything but wine.

"Nice ring, you stinker. When were you going to tell me?" Sally teases Jack.

"You like it?"

"It's gorgeous, prettier than a stick of soft butter on steamed corn."

"Why are we all standing outside in this air? Come in, everybody," I said, climbing my front steps.

"Good idea, Halsey, and keep yours and your dog's nose away from the fire investigation."

I turned in the direction of the voice and saw the owner was none other than our neighborhood gum-shoe. His car was parked in front of Marisol's house; this was undoubtedly the closest that he could get to the scene.

"Can't stay away can you, Augie?"

"It's for your own good; they are taking a good hard look at Enrico and Isabella's business and their actions leading up to the fire. They strongly suspect arson by the way the fire went up so fast. Someone started it, and to find the culprit they need to find out who stood to benefit the most from going out of business."

"Well it isn't the Brunos, Augie. They just went into a joint venture with the winery, opening up a whole new customer base for their delicious food." Sally, who towered over Augie, was all up in his face.

"Good to know," he replied, standing his ground.

"I hoped that you'd be on our side, Augie." I really was disappointed.

"I am on the side of right and wrong. I am on the side of the law!"

"Geez, Augustus, you're giving the family a bad name. Even a Boy Scout bites the head off a worm every once in a while."

I stared at Marisol, wondering if she was speaking from experience.

"You have all girls, Marisol, so when exactly were you hanging around Boy Scouts?" I said to her while opening my front door.

"I used to teach fencing."

"Where the heck did you learn that?"

"Old Errol Flynn movies."

* * *

"So, arson huh? That's a scary thought."

Jack and I were enjoying a bottle of Bonny Doon grenache after going for a relaxing evening dip in the pool. When I got home, I'd taken a thirty-minute shower and then I'd used an expensive, fragrant lotion to stamp out any remnant of a smoky smell, but I still felt gritty and, frankly, violated. I couldn't get my last image of Roberto, covered with a sheet, out of my head. Perhaps I was seeking a womb-like refuge in which to float away my memories of the day.

Bardot didn't care what the excuse was, she couldn't be happier that her two favorite people were in *her* pool. We'd taken turns racing her to the bottom of the pool to retrieve toys, and she'd won each time. She had finally resigned herself to the fact that we were done diving for the night and was stretched out on a chaise looking to the sky for shooting stars.

"Do you think Bardot actually smelled Roberto from that far away? I mean I know she liked him, because she made that clear every time I visited with Isabella at the pizza parlor. He'd pay her special attention and slip her a pepperoni."

Jack was grinning from ear to ear.

"What?"

He just kept grinning.

"Oh no, is that silly smile because I said 'slip her a pepperoni'?"

Now he was laughing.

"You are such a child."

"I'm just trying to cheer you up."

I couldn't help but crack a smile.

"But to answer your question . . . possibly. Scientists

believe that a dog's sense of smell could be up to a million times greater than ours. They can even sniff out elements that aren't detected by sophisticated technology."

"Wow, I wonder if she can smell winning lottery numbers."

"Bardot's wet schnozz can trap scent particles and give her information about them."

"Like what?"

"Well, first you need to understand that dogs use each nostril for different purposes. One is for breathing and one is for scenting. So with one sniff air is sent back to the lungs and the scent is diverted to the back of the nose."

"All of this is going on even when she is smelling another dog's butt?"

"Especially then. At the back of the nose they have these things called turbinates, which are full of scent receptors. We have them too, but they are not nearly as well developed. As Bardot sends a sniff back to the turbinates, the receptors send electrical impulses to her brain. And it stands to reason that the longer a dog's nose the more turbinates it will have."

"Which is why pugs make lousy hunting dogs." I'm proud of my powers of deduction.

"Among other reasons." Jack took a sip of wine before continuing. "Now add to this the fact that Bardot has a large olfactory bulb in her brain, and you've got a dog with extraordinary scenting ability."

I could tell that Jack was proud of himself.

"You are the dog nose whisperer, honey. But I'd still like to know if Bardot could smell all the way to the fire."

"I knew you wouldn't give up on that . . . more wine?" He poured while he thought.

"It's not that black-and-white, babe. Dogs like Bardot not only take in lots of scents, but they are also able to separate a scent they recognize from a thousand other ones. Like in a truckload of oranges, she can detect the one rotten one. Or in an Olympic-size swimming pool, she'd be able to locate a half tea-spoon of sugar. So it is not just about distance but about how they process the information being sent to their brain."

I got out of the pool, grabbed a towel, and joined Bardot on the chaise.

Maybe the stars will give me the answer . . .

"Okay, okay." Jack laughed and got out as well. "If we were in a court of law, I would tell them that a number of factors impact a dog's ability to detect scents. Weather, wind direction, the type of scent, and the dog's training are the main ones. In Bardot's case, she's been well trained in scent tracking, so that puts her way up there in ability. Today was clear with a nice breeze, so that also works in our favor. Labs have been recorded detecting unique scents at a distance of one-point-two miles, and I've heard of cadaver dogs that can identify a decaying body buried eighty feet underwater."

"Wow, if only we could get her to talk!"

"Maybe we can."

I looked at Jack for clues to what he meant by that. He smiled, and just before he spoke we heard: "Do you know what time it is? I almost died today, I need my sleep."

Like a Whac-A-Mole contestant, Marisol's head popped up above the fence separating our properties.

"You didn't almost die, Marisol, and since when do you sleep?"

"Not when you're out here getting drunk and having a wild party."

I surveyed our scene. Bardot and I were on the chaise, Jack sat on the grass beside us, and there were no extra lights on and no music. I quickly looked around for something resembling a mallet.

"Besides, you didn't need to know all that stuff from Jack. I already told you Bardie's nose knows. And by the way, she talks to me."

Chapter Four

The next day it was back to work for me. All of my mystery-solving shenanigans barely kept me out of jail and did little for my business and bank account. Even as I tried to focus, I couldn't get it out of my mind that Jack never did get around to telling me what he meant by "getting Bardot to talk." I wonder what he meant by that. Marisol had ruined the mood in more ways than one, and he'd gone home shortly after she popped her nosy head over the fence.

One more new client would take some of the pressure off and keep me out of trouble. I started combing through the tech newsgroups I subscribe to for a lead.

There wasn't much that interested me or was worth the time and effort, but then something caught my eye:

Liza Gilhooly Commercial Real Estate—RFP for website, including property database, inquiry capture, dynamic photo feeds, and rental calculator.

I'd seen her signs on storefronts and small office buildings around Mar Vista, and I'm all for helping out local women in business, so I downloaded the proposal form for this project.

The questions all seemed straightforward enough, but something made me decide that I was better off going to her office and introducing myself. She was close enough to walk, so I grabbed Bardot and we headed out.

Who doesn't love a visit from an adorable puppy?

Our route necessitated that we pass by the fire-ravaged strip mall. The sidewalk was all cordoned off with police tape, but there were a few inches of curb that were still accessible, so Bardot and I practiced our balance beam exercises. If returning to the scene of the crime bothered Bardot, she didn't show it. There were lots of odors to smell and she was taking inventory. I paused in front of the charred remains of Rico's Pizza. Nothing was recognizable any more—not the red and green neon sign that hung in the window, none of the white subway tiles that lined the walls, not even their heavy metal pizza oven was really discernible from the ashes. That had been some hot fire, and thinking back to the sequence of events it got hot very quickly. That must be why the arson inspectors were called in.

I tried to reason why Enrico and Isabella would have set the fire, and I couldn't come up with a plausible scenario. Sure they worked very hard, but they took two weeks off every summer to visit relatives in Italy.

I also doubt that it was for the insurance money; it would be a long time before they saw any payout, and they seemed to be doing just fine financially. But you never really know.

"Total bummer, isn't it?"

I turned and saw that the question came from a

twentysomething guy in board shorts and a tank. He had that dark caramel tan that you get from surfing every day, and his sandy blond hair was tied in a top knot and the sides were shaved close to the scalp.

Justin Bieber called, he wants his vibe back . . .

"It's just so sad," I replied. "Did you like to get pizza from here too?"

"A slice a day."

"Wow, you must be Rico's best customer."

"And neighbor . . . I had the auto parts store two doors down."

He pointed toward a section of the mall in about the center of the building.

"Oh gosh, I'm so sorry. I'm Halsey by the way."

"Brandon," he said, and extended his tattooed hand.

"Were you here yesterday when it started?"

"Me? No, Sundays are really slow and besides the barrels were bitchin'."

I assumed he was talking about surfing since he punctuated his statement by making the shaka sign with his thumb and little finger. I gave him a knowing nod, hoping to convince him that I was a fellow wave rider and fervent studier of the tide charts.

"Are you going to re-build? I mean once everything is settled with insurance."

"Nah, I inherited this business from my grand-father. He lived nearby and worked the store until he dropped."

What a quaint way of remembering him . . .

"By the time I got it, the store was well on its way towards tanking. Nobody tinkers with their own cars anymore, and if you do need something the chains like Pep Boys can sell parts much cheaper and still make a profit."

"Sounds like you didn't have a fighting chance."

"Don't get me wrong, at the beginning I tried everything to get it back up and going. Promos, sales, demos, the whole nine. Mostly I'd get old geezers coming in to shoot the sh–"—he paused—"the breeze."

I knew it, deep down Brandon had some manners buried.

He slipped under the tape and headed into his store.

"Is it safe for you to be going in there?"

"The fire's all out, and I just gotta look for one thing. I'll be fine, Halsey."

I wondered what he thought would have survived the fire since even the pizza oven burned. I was tempted to follow him in, but I hadn't been invited to join him in the charred mess, and I certainly didn't want to run into any fire inspectors.

"What are you doing here?"

Curses, Inspector Mason.

I hadn't noticed the fire department van pull up, and now I had some 'splaining to do.

"I'm on my way to a client meeting." I pointed down the street to a small office building. "What are you doing here?"

"This area is restricted and dangerous . . . can't you see the tape?"

"My dog and I are standing outside the tape, but you might want to tell the owner of the auto parts store. He just went in to retrieve something."

Mason took off after Brandon. I felt a pang of guilt telling on him, but the inspector would have seen Brandon anyway. I knew that I should move on now, but I really wanted to ask Mason about the Brunos and try to convince him that they could not have started the fire. I wasn't sure how he'd take the information about Bardot's advanced olfactory sense, but it was certainly worth a try. Moments later he returned to the sidewalk.

"I don't know what you're talking about, there was no one in there."

"That's odd, he introduced himself, his name is Brandon, and I watched him go in there. Could he have left out the back?"

"He could, but why would he? The front is clear, but there is lots of debris blocking the back. He'd have to climb over it to get out through the small opening."

"Brandon told me that he was a surfer. Maybe he went that way for the challenge."

"Or maybe he didn't want you to see what he was taking out of there, Halsey."

Mason eyed me while processing this information. He struck me as an intrinsically suspicious guy. My guess is that on Halloween when kids come to his door, he takes his time weighing the options of "Trick" or "Treat" before committing.

"Are you done with Rico and Isabella now? Have you ruled them out as arson suspects?"

"We haven't even declared the *fire* as being arson, let alone compiled a list of suspects. These are meticulous investigations that follow strict protocol and require time to conduct. Which is why you need to stay clear of this and let us do our jobs."

He said this with a conviction that left no wiggle room, so Bardot and I turned our backs to Mason and headed on down the street.

* * *

Liza Gilhooly Commercial Real Estate was on the ground floor of a three-story building. Photos of commercial buildings for sale and their specs peeked out the window at me from a ledge. It was fairly dark inside. I figured that I was standing in front of the only source of natural light for the space. I was about to turn around and head home when the glass and metal-framed door opened partway, triggering a cheery tea bell attached to the door closer at the top. A woman's head popped out; this was my week to be surprised by women's heads popping up, I guess. Hopefully, this one wasn't as nutty as "Whac-A-Mole" Marisol.

"Hi! Come on in, I'm Liza. And bring this beautiful blondie with you. I'm sure I can scare up a dog cookie somewhere."

Bardot didn't need to be asked twice and practically dragged me into the office.

"Please, have a seat," Liza Gilhooly directed me. "Give me a sec to find those biscuits."

I had a chance to study the Realtor while she opened and closed drawers and moved stacks of papers around to locate a tasty biscuit. I'm going to peg her at around sixty. Her dyed blond hair was loosely held atop her head with a pair of chopsticks, and she moved with surprising agility in a turquoise, bell-bottomed pantsuit. Her makeup brought out her pleasant features, and I tried to imagine her as a two-episode love interest on *The Six Million Dollar Man* in her day.

"Aha! Here we go."

She produced two faded bone-shaped items that looked like they had been there since the Nixon administration. Bardot didn't mind and after chomping gave Liza her most genial smile.

"Thank you," I said. "I'm Halsey. I actually live nearby on Rose Avenue."

"Liza Gilhooly, and this is—?"

"Bardot, as in Brigitte."

Bardot performed a tail-wagging twirl to show off her superstar-ness.

"So what sort of business do you run, Halsey, and how much space are you going to need?"

I quickly explained the reason for my visit, dashing her hopes that I was heading up another Google-size company to set up shop in the area. To her credit Liza hardly altered her expression.

"Perfect! Everyone had been sending me these long proposals, and I've been stressing about how I'd find the time to read them all, let alone understand them. I'm a bit of a Luddite you see."

Liza feigned shame, but I could tell that she was proud of using the term "Luddite," meaning someone who eschews technology.

"Is this your family?" I gave a framed photo of at least three generations of people a closer look.

"Hah! No, I'm an only child and never married. But some of my clients are big family people so I put that photo out. If they ask I'll tell them the truth, but more often than not they just assume."

Just then the phone rang, and she pulled one multitasking chopstick from her bun and used it to depress the button, thereby keeping her fingernail extensions intact.

"Yes, this is Liza Gilhooly," she said into the phone

while holding the chopstick in the air instead of her index finger to let me know that she'd be just a second. "I see, I'm so sorry for your loss. What sort of business was this? A drugstore! Of course, I've shopped there many, many times. Listen, may I get your name and number and ring you back in a few? I'm with a business associate and I don't want to keep her waiting."

Business associate? Does that mean that I've got the job?

She scribbled down the caller's information, which was quite a feat since for this task the chopstick was of no help. After she hung up, she shook her head slowly.

"Did you happen to see that fire up the street yesterday, Halsey?"

I nodded. "Not only that. Bardot and I were *in* it!"

Liza sat up ramrod straight.

"The person that just called owned the drugstore that burned to the ground. They want to start fresh and get out from under those smarmy investors who own the mall."

Now I was sitting ramrod straight.

"Sounds like you have quite a story to tell me about them," I encouraged her.

"Seems like you do too, Halsey. Shall we roll for who goes first?"

Liza reached under her desk and presented me with one of a pair of neon pink fuzzy dice.

Chapter Five

It was Wine Club Tuesday, and we were gathered at Aimee's house for the imbibing and imparting of information. Aimee is the ultimate hostess to the point where you wish that she'd just sit down for a bit and enjoy her guests.

She and her doctor boyfriend Tom have been doing some renovations on their home, including new kitchen cabinets and adding a heavy, mission-style round oak dining table, which was where we had all gathered. Since we were all still recovering from the effects of the fire, we were eating and pouring light today. Sally made her "drunken tomatoes"—vodka-infused little gems with sea salt and coarse black pepper.

What? Vodka is made from potatoes, so it is just another vegetable.

Aimee had gone Mediterranean on us and laid out an impressive tray of three kinds of olives, roasted red pepper and artichoke tapenade with grilled pita bread, mini spanakopita squares, several hummus dips, and feta and watermelon skewers. Peggy and I contributed the wine and today chose to serve an

Argiolas Costamolino Vermentino from Sardinia, Italy (my choice), and Peggy went with a Heitz Grignolino rosé from Napa Valley, California.

The Vermentino is a white wine grape that has a lemony acidity. It is aromatic, light, and refreshing. We've been known to go through a number of bottles without even counting. Peggy's Grignolino is a red Italian grape with a light, tangy touch of cranberry and red currant. Yum!

"I am just sick about Rico and Isabella's loss, and poor Roberto, let's take a moment to remember him," Aimee said after we'd toasted and let the first grape elixir wake up our taste buds.

"It is really a shock, and to think that the inspectors are looking to pin this on them. We're just going to have to nip that in the bud." Peggy looked around the table challenging us to the task.

This wasn't just wishful thinking on Peggy's part because, in addition to enlisting us, she did have some friends with real muscle and investigative pull. You see, as a young woman she served briefly with the CIA, and by that I mean she spied on Russians flying in and out of the Santa Monica Airport. And at close to ninety she still had it.

"I'm thinking that the best way that we can help the Brunos is to throw as many credible SODDIs into the mix as possible." Before I could go on, Aimee chimed in.

"What kind of sodies? We have some really yummy root beer, but it comes from a fountain, we don't have it in cans."

"Sweet Jesus and pass the macaroni. She said S-O-D-D-I; it's a legal defense term, honey, and stands for 'some other dude did it.' Great idea, Halsey, but how do we come up with the dudes?"

Sally had once again astounded me with her expressions.

"We may already have two."

That got everyone's attention in a hurry. I told them about my encounter with Brandon, the surfer boy and failing auto parts shop inheritor.

"What do you think he was going back into those awful ruins for? Gosh, maybe it was a photo of his dear departed grandfather," Aimee suggested, and cued the waterworks.

"He didn't seem all too broken up about the loss of a familial elder when he told me the story."

"This kind of sleuthing is right up my alley," Peggy declared. "Or should I say my old friends' and associates' alley from The Company."

"Seems like a bit of a long shot, but if you need my help, Peggy, I'm all yours."

While stellar of Sally to offer assistance, I know for a fact that their research forays often roll right into a mini Wine Club à deux.

"Great!"

"You said you had two sodas, Halsey?"

I wasn't going to correct Aimee again. She looked so earnest in her desire to help that I didn't want to dampen her spirit.

"You are a really good listener, Aimee. The second one is a real lead to follow up on."

I explained how I ended up in Liza Gilhooly's office and added that before I left I'd been awarded the job of building her commercial real estate website.

Momentum then stopped for congratulatory toasts and more wine. When everyone settled down again, I continued.

"While I was with her, she got a call from the owners of the drugstore that was in the fire asking her to help find them another location. They told her that they wanted nothing further to do with the owners of their old building regardless of how fast they rebuilt."

"Aha, do we have a not-so-accidental-fire situation here? And I don't mean the Brunos." Peggy was grinning at the prospect of catching a thief.

"It's a possibility. Liza says that the owners are a group of investors that keep their holdings and real estate history very close to their vest. But Liza, who's been around the rodeo a few years, remembers the same group buying up street-level retail locations like crazy in the mid- to late eighties. They called themselves the Provident Commerce Group of Mar Vista, and back then they were giving out loans and rental contracts like green beer on Saint Paddy's Day. But then the nineties hit and the market tanked."

"I remember that," Sally said as she thought back. "I was working for a cardiologist, Dr. Fenzel, and we suddenly got very busy."

"Did your new client have anything else to say about this group? How did they fare during the slump?"

"That's the curious part. Liza says that almost from one day to the next all the signs disappeared from the buildings they owned, and no one saw or heard from them for the next ten years."

"Oh wow, and what happened to the businesses that were in their buildings? Was everybody okay?"

This hit close to home for Aimee. Her frozen yogurt shop was in a nearby strip mall, and a couple of years ago she had faced her own scary issues with the building and another tenant two doors down from her.

"Unfortunately, that's where Liza dropped the scent. She took a two-week vacation in Maui, met a Frenchman who claimed to have a fashion house in Paris, and she had a wild romance until her money ran out. It seems that his had run out before she'd hit the island and he was on his third or fourth "love at first sight." It took Liza a while to build her finances and business back up, so she doesn't remember hearing anything about the Provident Commerce Group until around 2003 or 2004 when their signs suddenly started reappearing."

"Curiouser and curiouser," Sally mused.

"Does Liza think that they set the fire?"

"She wouldn't go that far, Peggy, which is why we should pick up the trail and see what we can learn about them."

"I can ask the owner of my building," Aimee offered. "He's really discrete and owes me one for the incident with the Jamaicans."

"Great, I'll do some investigating as well. It looks like we may need to have another Wine Club this week."

"Aw, well, it's for a good cause." Sally raised her glass and we all came together in a toast.

"What's all this about investigating and Wine Clubs? Are you lasses up to your old tricks without me?"

"Penelope!" We all cheered again before she gave us a round of kisses.

"I had to drop nearby to handle some paperwork with Rico and Isabella and thought I'd walk down Rose Avenue and listen for the sound of glasses clinking. You girls will toast to anything." She laughed heartily and accepted a glass from Aimee.

Peggy and Sally brought her up to speed on what we knew.

"I think that Andrew knows that Brandon fellow. He loves to surf too and made an excuse to go out every time he visited Rico's Pizza. In fact, I'm not sure which came first, the reciprocal deal for pizza and wine or the surfing buddies."

"Then he may know what Brandon was looking for in his burned-down place." Aimee got excited again, and her cheeks blossomed into candy apples.

"Maybe we should take a different approach," I said, quickly jumping in. "After all, he had every right to recover what he could. Brandon's under enough stress . . . he needs his surfing time with Andrew to relax and sort things out."

Peggy caught my drift and said, "Halsey's right . . . we don't know anything. But if Andrew does mention the fire or his buddy, it would be great if you could recount back to us what was said, Penelope."

"Detective Lieutenant Master Penelope reporting for duty." She grinned and saluted us. She was clearly still in the honeymoon stage of her new life, and nothing was going to bring her down.

"How is the loss of the pizza parlor going to impact your Fall Harvest Party in the tasting room?"

"I worried about that too, Sally, but Isabella seems to think that she can bring all the ingredients to the winery and assemble the pies on site. Andrew told me that she came up for a look-see a few days ago, before the fire, and fell in love with the place. He suspects that she'd be perfectly happy running a pizza parlor just for our guests. She told him she just needs a very hot oven. We do have an outdoor brick fireplace and Malcolm downloaded plans to convert it to a pizza oven. His guys think that they can get it ready in time."

"Fabulous!" Aimee started another toast.

The neighborhood was quiet on my short walk home as is par for the course. Upon arriving back at my house, I spotted Marisol pulling some grass out from between my front white rose bushes. She often disguises her need for information or a favor with a random act of kindness that she quickly abandons when she gets what she wants.

"Have you decided to take up the lawn and landscape profession, Marisol?"

"This is an eyesore; you're bringing down the whole neighborhood."

I sat down on my front step and invited her into my "office."

"How may I help you today, Mrs. Marisol Ysabel Rosario Priscila Cordoba?"

That is her full name, but I might have been a tad over served at Wine Club.

"You need to fix this. I miss my chicken wings from Rico's already."

"In what way do you think that Rico's burning down was my fault, Marisol?"

"Something's always your fault, although probably

not this time. But you can make it so they open a new one right away."

"And how do you think that I can do that exactly? You're the one with the witchcraft and magic wands."

"You need to prove that Rico and Isabella didn't have anything to do with the fire. They get their insurance money, and I get my wings. But we need Bardie's help."

I groused inside from her assault on Bardot's given name.

"Why do I have a sneaking suspicion that you already have a plan, Marisol?"

"I've been reading up and talking to people. I know how these things start, and on Sunday when most of the businesses were closed this couldn't have been no accident."

"Doesn't that reinforce that it was the Brunos then? They were working."

"Not if we find out that the point of origin was not in their restaurant. That's what Bardie—"

I gave her a look from hell.

"Bardot needs to tell us. We have to go at night. I've got Friday open, or I could do Sunday, but it would have to be after the Dionne Warwick special."

With that she toddled off. My front lawn was now strewn with long grass blades and weeds that I would have to clean up. I channeled my inner Sally.

You better give your heart to Jesus, Marisol, because your butt is mine!

Chapter Six

I woke up charged with energy, had breakfast at my desk—an English crumpet with smooth peanut butter and a cup of tea—and was ready to start laying out Liza Gilhooly's website. Which instantly got me thinking about the Provident Commerce Group, and that led to a sidetracked online search for the entity.

After being baited by several sites that claimed to have everything I wanted to know only to stop halfway and tell me I needed to pay $29.99 a month to continue, I decided that a different approach was in order.

I called Isabella and asked her what she could tell me about her landlords—the owners of the strip mall.

"We never see them," she told me. "Our rent checks are sent to a bank, and if we have any issues with the unit, we have the name of a manager to call. But he is never available . . . he manages a bunch of buildings in the Valley and usually by the time he calls us back we have fixed the problem ourselves. And footed the bill, which we can't afford to keep doing."

"That's annoying. Who signed the lease on their side? Do you have a name of someone in this real estate group?"

I heard Isabella sigh.

"That's the thing, Enrico is looking for our copy now. We've talked to our insurance adjuster, but he needs to talk to the owners. As usual the manager is not calling us back."

"Hmm, that doesn't sound good, and I suppose they have a deposit from you as well?"

"Two months."

I don't like any of this.

"Is it possible that the lease burned in the fire?"

"I guess so. We try to keep all our important papers at the bank, but the lease wasn't in the box. Enrico is searching our house for it."

"Okay, hang in there, and you know how to find me if you need anything."

I was just about to hang up when I had a thought.

"Isabella, wait. Do you know that kid Brandon who ran the auto parts store?"

She let out a dry laugh.

"Yes, he was running that store, all the way into the ground if you ask me."

"Really? He claims that he tried everything to market his products and turn it around."

"Maybe from atop a surfboard he did, but I never saw it. Brandon and Roberto were pals. They seemed to spend a lot of time together when they weren't working."

"You mean on the water?"

"No, Roberto didn't care for the ocean, may he rest in peace. It was more like they were constantly working on some 'get rich quick' scheme. When deliveries were slow, I'd see them out back smoking and talking in low voices. If I took the trash out, they would immediately stop their conversation and wait until I went back in the restaurant. Occasionally, when Rico was on a break, I'd join them for a cigarette and the conversation would always turn to music or girls. Innocent stuff like that."

Interesting, including the fact that they smoked.

"If you're looking for Brandon's surfing buddies, you'd have to go to Venice Beach most mornings. Or maybe talk to Malcolm's cousin Andrew. I hear that he's a big surfer, and usually after he was finished here, he'd walk up to Brandon's place and the two would talk for hours. Roberto and Brandon thought of Andrew as a role model. He had money, a cool job. Me? I thought that the guy was a little too young to think so highly of himself. What is the saying . . . too big for his britches?"

"Yes, that's the phrase."

"Anyway, while they were loafing around, Rico and I were working hard every day to keep things going. Rico turns sixty-five in three years and I'm not far behind."

I tucked that bit of info into the file cabinets of my mind, thanked Isabella for her time, and repeated my offer of help. I pulled out a yellow index card from my desk drawer and wrote down two names:

Brandon (need last name)

Provident Commerce Group (need any and all names!)

"Hey, kiddo, what're you up to?"

Sally entered into my office with that healthy glow of having just walked one thousand steps. She went into my little kitchen and grabbed herself a water out of the mini fridge.

"I just got off the phone with Isabella. She told me some unsettling things about life in their strip mall."

I filled Sally in.

"So Brandon lied to you. He wasn't trying to save his business, but what would be the point? He certainly didn't need to impress you . . . for all he knew you were just a passerby and he'd never see you again." Sally picked up a wooden tennis racquet from my collection and practiced her forehand. I bet that she'd been a formidable competitor in her day. She had the elegance and grace of Venus Williams.

"Exactly." I nodded to Sally and got out of the way of her big swing. "Maybe he was practicing his story. You know how they say when someone is lying about their testimony they tend to tell it the same way time after time? And if they are telling the truth it will vary slightly with each recount?"

"I hadn't heard that, but it makes sense." Sally spotted a tennis ball by the pool and walked out the French doors to retrieve it.

I followed behind her. "You need to quit watching PBS so much, Sally, and come over to the dark side. Immerse yourself in a little *Bull* and *Law & Order*."

She laughed. "Maybe I should." After thinking for a moment, she asked, "How well did you know Roberto?" She bounced the ball to test its freshness. I sat down on the steps to my office and let my face catch some sun.

"Not very well. He was little more than a kid and we had nothing in common. But even when he was working, he always seemed distracted and a little arrogant to me. Like in a 'If you only knew, I'm better than this,' kind of way. I feel guilty saying that about the dead, but it's the impression I got of Roberto."

"Hey, this is your BFF you're talking to, I completely understand." My best friend forever gave a quick nod.

"Thanks. Where are you going with this, Sally?"

"I was just thinking that maybe Roberto and Brandon were in on starting the fire together. Perhaps to just burn the auto parts store and something went terribly wrong, the fire spread and Roberto was trapped inside the burning building? We are talking about insurance money here."

"That's a plausible theory. Roberto may have needed an attitude adjustment, but I know he respected the Brunos and I can't believe he would willingly do anything to hurt them."

"It's a different world out there today, although I doubt that most of these kids even see it, they're so focused on their tiny phone screens. I told you that I've been giving CPR classes at the church, haven't I, Halsey?"

"I remember you mentioning something about cardiopulmonary resuscitation instruction; how's that going?"

"The class is mostly filled with the people that are probably going to need CPR sooner rather than later. A bunch of old fogies. But I was pleased last Sunday to see four guys about Roberto's age in attendance."

"Did you ask what brought them in?"

"In a round-about way I did. I asked if there was anything in particular that they wanted me to show them, and this one fellow said that his kid sister had a pool accident and he just froze. Luckily, there was someone else on site to administer CPR."

"Hmm, you know how people say that millennials are the me, me, me generation? That they think that they deserve everything?"

Sally gave me a firm nod in agreement.

"What if the truth is the opposite? And their arrogance is just a defense mechanism for feelings of inadequacy? Think about it, everything they say and do is judged immediately by their peers and their families on social media."

"You're right. At least when I made a bone-head move as a kid I could go and hide in my room and leaf through my granddaddy's encyclopedia of infectious diseases."

I had no rebound to that statement from Sally.

She tossed the tennis ball in the air and went through the motions of serving, letting the ball drop back down at her feet.

We both were lost in thought for a moment. Bardot ambled up to us from the chaise lounge by the pool. I assumed that she had put all the squirrels in their place and was relinquishing patrol for a while.

Sally went through another serve motion and this time hit the ball, aiming for the fence that separated my yard from Marisol's. It sailed high and over, and we heard the sound of pottery breaking.

"I'm suing you, Halsey!" came a yell from the other side of the fence.

"Bardot, you know a lot more than you're saying, don't you? Don't you?"

Sally had a special voice she used when talking to Bardot—it's a habit people fall into with babies and pets that I've never understood. After all Bardot doesn't bark slower or softer when she is among friends of the human variety.

Although I must admit that Bardot loved it and was now on her back at Sally's feet, legs splayed wide for all the world to see her lady parts.

"Sorry to interrupt this canine love fest," said Jack, coming in the street entrance of my office. "Hello, wifey-to-be." He gave me a kiss.

"Not if you're going to call me 'wifey.'"

"Sorry. Hi, Sally. How are you doing?"

I looked over and saw that Bardot had suddenly sat up straight and at attention for Jack.

You're such a teacher's pet . . .

"I've only got a minute, but I thought you'd find this interesting," Jack teased us.

"What have you got, big guy?" This had gotten Sally's attention.

"It's about the fire. I was working with my friend Mark early this morning . . . we're training a couple of new dogs. Mark's with the DEA; he and I go way back," Jack said for Sally's benefit.

"Did he say that there were drugs involved with the strip mall fire?"

"In a way, Halsey. The Drug Enforcement Agency was called when it was reported that the drugstore's safe was missing from the scene."

"Maybe it burned to almost nothing like the pizza oven?"

"Same question I asked, Sally. But the owners of the drugstore have paperwork showing that the safe was guaranteed to be fireproof for heat up to seventeen hundred degrees for about an hour."

"What if the safe didn't live up to its claims?"

Someone has to be the skeptic.

"Mark says that's unlikely. This safe was made with something called 'insulite'; it has passed UL tests with flying colors and is the preferred material for vaults used by financial institutions."

"Interesting . . . good work, honey. I'm guessing

that since Mark is now involved the contents of this safe were of the pharmaceutical kind?"

Jack pointed his index finger to his nose, indicating that my hunch was correct. Bardot saw that as some sort of doggie command hand signal and offered up a "down," "rollover," and "crouch" pose to cover her bases.

"Jack, what was the size of this safe? Could it be moved by a couple of young, strong guys?"

"Who do you have in mind, Sally?" Jack gave her a wink.

We waited for him to continue.

"Okay, never mind. The safe would have been heavy but movable. I'm told that it was used mostly to house the opioids in their inventory. The good news is that if whoever stole the drugs goes to sell them on the street that at least they are legit and not synthetic. But naturally Mark would rather take possession of them first. You ladies have someone in mind for this theft?"

Sally was about to speak when I interrupted.

"It's a long shot, and we really have no evidence at all. We're just throwing spaghetti on the wall to see if it sticks."

Jack squinted his eyes at me to show his suspicion.

"Cross my heart," I said while deliberately running my hand in an "X" pattern over both breasts.

Jack was no longer squinting.

The ring of his cell phone broke in, and he grabbed it out of his pocket to check the caller ID.

"Darn, I've got to boogie, babe, I've got a crazy day. I'll call you when I can. Bye, Sally!"

"Well, that was an interesting bit of news," Sally looked at me.

"It sure was. Who knows what those drugs could fetch on the street? I remember reading something saying that Oxy is going for a crazy fourteen times what it sells for in a drugstore."

"What? That could make me lose my religion!" Sally looked at her pedometer, exited, and continued her step routine.

I made myself a second cup of tea, drank it, relaxed, and then managed to herd my thoughts into laying out Liza Gilhooly's site in the afternoon, which made me feel like I hadn't totally wasted the day musing about "kids these days." I was hoping to get started on it right away while my mind was focused, so I gave her a call.

"Halsey, what a nice surprise! Is my website finished?" She followed her silly question with a deep, extended belly laugh.

"In a way, Liza. I've got all the technical specs and site map worked out and was wondering when you had time to go over everything."

"Wow, I was just kidding. You really are fast. Hmm, I've got a couple of showings this evening . . . hey, want to meet sometime tomorrow?"

"Perfect; ten work for you?"

"Sure does unless one of my showings turns into an extended showing if you get my drift." On came that Liza laugh again.

"Quick question before I let you go, Liza. You were telling me the other day about this Provident Commerce Group. Do you remember the names of any of the partners?"

"Oh, sweetie, you're asking me to dust off a lot of cobwebs in my thinking cap. It's also possible that what they told me was a total fabrication. I'm going to need to work on this for a bit. I'll call you if I get a brain burp. Toodles."

I wasn't sure how much help Liza would be if she regained her memory, but I wasn't about to give up on the owners of the strip mall. Too many things didn't add up or sounded very unusual. Why didn't anyone know their names? Why did they hide behind managers and shill company lawyers? I made a note to find out how much rent the Brunos had been paying. I was about to call it a day and go for a swim with Bardot when the great Aretha Franklin sang out as my ringtone with her rendition of, "I Say a Little Prayer." I figured Liza was calling back to tell me that she'd had a "brain burp" as she called it.

"You remembered a name?" I'd answered, not bothering to check the caller ID.

"What name? This is Inspector Mason."

Ugh.

"I thought that you were someone else calling."

"What name are you asking someone to remember, Halsey?"

I was sliding down the rabbit hole and needed to end this.

"How can I help you, Inspector? I assume that you called for a reason. You are aware that I am affianced?"

That shut him up for a moment.

"I want to follow up on your conversation with this Brandon guy," he said. "I'd like to take your statement and record exactly what you saw and what was said."

"Okay, ask away."

"I'm afraid it has to be a little more formal than a phone call. If you give me your address I can stop by within the hour."

Ew, that wasn't going to happen. It was getting dark out, no bueno.

"I'm all booked up today and I don't really like to have visitors. My dog can be very possessive and protective of me."

"You know I've met your dog, Halsey?" Inspector Mason paused for a beat. "Are you able to come down to the firehouse? It is very close to where you live."

"How do you know where I live?"

"Anytime that is convenient, like between nine and ten tomorrow morning."

Convenient my butt. Then I had an idea.

"I have an important meeting at ten so whatever you need to know has to happen in less than an hour. I'll see you then, Inspector Mason."

I hung up before he could argue to change the meeting time.

It was then that I did something that I was most certainly going to regret.

"Marisol, I need your help," I said after I'd dialed.

Chapter Seven

The next morning, right at nine, I parked across the street from Fire Station 62 and watched an engine back into one of two large garage doors. As expected, the vehicle was pristine, the cherry red so polished that I could see my reflection in the side of the truck from thirty feet away. The driver waved to me from out his window. Ah, I was entering the world of happy, helpful people.

I'd gotten a text from Liza Gilhooly about an hour before, asking if we could postpone our meeting until Monday. She said that she was busy with an offer she needed to get inked. I realized that her business leases and deeds would always take top priority.

This station looked relatively new compared to some of the relics I've seen around Venice; it was modern, sleek, but inviting. The façade of the entry to the lobby was made of corrugated tin siding that had been painted what I'd call an "Easter purple." The front door was locked but to the right was a lighted red button. A strip of paper with the words PLEASE RING BELL was taped beside it.

I did as I was told. *Something I do on rare occasions.*

In moments the door opened, and I heard a man say, "There's no one here." I hadn't expected the big door to open so wide. In order to avoid being hit by it, I had to keep moving into the wall until I was actually wedged between the outside of the door and the right side of the building's façade.

"I'm behind the door." I felt like a dork.

I saw two heads appear around the open door and smile at me. They were both in their twenties I guessed. One was tall, dark, and handsome and one was tall, blond, and handsome. Take your pick.

"Hi, I'm Halsey, and I was told to meet Inspector Mason here."

"Come on in. I'm Cody and this is Phillip. We're paramedics, but the captain's engine just pulled into the apparatus bay and he should be able to help you."

"Thank you. Is there any chance that I could get a quick tour of the station?" As a teenager I'd practiced the look I gave them in the mirror for hours each day. It was the one where I smile with closed lips, putting slight emphasis on my right cheek where the dimple is more pronounced. Simultaneously, I ever so slightly raise my left eyebrow to give my expression some counterbalance and allure. And since they were both well over six feet tall I had to raise my eyes up for eye contact.

Works every time.

"Sure," they said in unison.

The lobby was cavernous . . . To the left a wide staircase ascended past a mural painted in the bright, saturated colors that I remember seeing at the strip mall fire. It depicts three firefighters climbing painted stairs that appear to be a continuation of the actual stairs of the station and into a doorway ablaze in orange fire. One of the men carries a working water hose. It is impressive and somber at the same time.

"Upstairs are the sleeping quarters," Phillip explained, following the direction that I was looking. "And in front of us is the pole that we use during night dispatches."

"Would you like to head up and take a look?"

How could I say "no" to dear Cody?

"I thought that you had a meeting at ten that you just can't miss?"

Cue the needle-scratching-record sound effect.

"Ah, Inspector Mason. These gentlemen were kind enough to give me a tour of the station while I waited for you to arrive for our nine-a.m. meeting. I've got just about thirty-five minutes now."

Never mind that my meeting had been postponed. A promise is a promise.

"I've been in the apparatus bay the entire time waiting for you, Halsey!"

"How would I have known that? I came into the lobby just like any other tax-paying citizen."

I heard snickers from my fire boys.

"Come on into the garage. I've set up in there and the captain is joining us."

Mason turned his back on me and started toward a side door.

I didn't budge.

"Are you coming?" he demanded.

"What is that word I'm waiting to hear, Cody?"

"Is it 'please'?"

"I think it is."

I literally could see smoke coming out of Inspector Mason's ears at this point and turned my attention to the pole, expecting firefighters to arrive on scene at any second.

Mason dropped his head and turned it to one shoulder in an effort to control his temper.

This is a man that didn't like to be scolded. Which led me to believe that he had been . . . a lot.

"Please." It was more than a whisper but sounded like it came from a sickly Keebler elf.

"Thanks, guys. If it's alright with you, I'll come back and finish that tour when I'm less pressed for time and aggravation."

"Sure!"

At that point a voice came over the loudspeaker system, and I could make out the words "paramedics" and part of an address.

"That's us," Phillip said, and they took off.

Inside my mind I quickly said a little prayer for their safety. *They're so young*.

Inspector Mason had already gone through the side door, and I followed suit.

The apparatus bay was cavernous but bright and sunny. Men were gathered around a waist-high platform that when I got nearer saw—embedded in the top—a laminated map of the Los Angeles area. The station captain introduced himself to me, since Inspector Mason still hadn't been able to put his hands on his misplaced manners.

"Thanks for coming down to help us, Ms. Halsey." Another firefighter that looked like the picture of kindness. The captain's warm face and smile made me promise myself to drink some of the station's water before I left. I could use some squeaky clean to rub off on me.

"Thank you, Captain, for keeping our Mar Vista community safe. Thank all of you," I added, addressing the few firefighters standing on each side of him.

"I'd like to go over two events that you witnessed. One on the day of the fire and the second when you encountered the owner of the auto parts store the next morning."

Inspector Mason really doesn't play well with others . . .

I nodded slightly and waited for him to ask his question. The noise of a second truck pulling in had distracted him. Mason walked out of the apparatus bay as he spoke, and I followed along with the others.

"Now this is important—"

"I assume so or I wouldn't be here." I couldn't resist.

The captain opened the door to his office, and we all settled at a small conference table. I did a quick check and didn't see any photos from home of a blushing bride or a passel of toddlers.

What? I'm just gathering information.

"When you arrived on the scene of the fire and before you ran into the building after your dog, tell me what and who you saw." Inspector Mason had assumed the position of power at the head of the table. The benevolent captain didn't seem to mind a bit.

I resisted saying all of that was in my previous statement, but I'd seen enough cop shows to know that he'd only make me repeat it. Plus, I had a new audience of lovely firefighters. I made my way around to their side of the table to face Inspector Mason, which made me feel instantly better.

"Bardot, that's my yellow Lab," I explained to my boys, "had been pulling me to the building all the way from Rose Avenue. When we arrived as close as we could be to the front of the strip mall, she thrust her nose in the air, took in a deep sampling, and yanked me toward the back of the burning structure. I'm pretty sure that's because she smelled Roberto."

Inspector Mason snickered, but my fire boys, as I now called them, tried to process this.

"What? You think that I have an unrestrained imagination that leads me to anthropomorphize my dog's thoughts and abilities?"

I stared at Mason and reminded myself to give Jack a back rub later as a thank-you for the information that I was about to impart.

"Clearly you don't know this, but Bardot is a highly trained scent tracker for CARA. Labs have been recorded to detect unique scents at a distance of one-point-two miles, and cadaver dogs can identify a decaying body buried eighty feet underwater."

I could see that Mason wasn't buying this, but the guys on my side of the table were rapt.

"Dogs like Bardot not only take in lots of scents, but they are also able to separate a scent they recognize from a thousand other ones. Like in a truckload of a thousand rotten eggs, she can detect the one fresh one." *I think that's what Jack said.* "But if you don't believe me, Inspector Mason, go ask a dog."

The guys laughed at that, and Mason was forced to move on.

"At any time that you were at the scene on the day of the fire did you see the gentleman that we now know as Brandon Dawson, owner of the auto parts store?"

I actually did want to help him with this. I knew I would be helping Isabella and Rico, and that was my goal. I took a good minute to run through the images of that day in my mind.

"This is difficult. Unlike Bardot I can't easily separate the sights and sounds of that day. For me what I remember is the scene of utter chaos and a rising panic as my mind tried to grasp the severity of the situation." I tried to focus on my memories from the back of the building.

"Take your time," the captain encouraged me, and placed a gentle hand on my shoulder.

"The parking area was soaked with water from the hoses, and I could see bright orange and red flames coming from the roof . . . and pitch-black smoke."

"The fire was set in the communal attic that stretched across the mall; that is the only way that you and your dog could have survived going in and out of the pizza parlor." The kind captain picked up the story. "It is not like you see in the movies or on TV. If a structure is engulfed from floor to ceiling, we can't go inside. We create a vertical vent for the fire to find the oxygen it needs and fight it from outside and above."

Mason gave the captain a look. I guessed that he didn't want me knowing the specifics of an ongoing investigation. I realized that the firefighter's job is to rescue victims and put out blazes. After that they are on to the next one. The job of an arsonist inspector is to figure out if the fire was set on purpose, and if so find and arrest the perpetrators. It doesn't nearly attract as much positive PR. Both jobs are vital, but I was starting to understand why Inspector Mason acted the way he did regarding public relations toward me. *Time to give him some slack.*

"I saw firefighters climbing ladders that were propped up against the back walls of the building and watched a giant ladder extend from a fire truck to way above the flames. A responder at the top held a hose and once in place turned on the water. People were standing all around watching them work, some from a safe distance away and some in questionable proximity. People had brought their pets, babies, and elders to the spectator arena. I remember that just before Bardot broke loose from me and ran into the building, I made eye contact with a blond-headed girl who couldn't have been more than eight years old. She was wearing a dress with cute bird illustrations on it, lacy anklet socks, and gold shoes. I remember thinking that this was no place for such a pretty little girl. But I don't remember seeing Brandon then or after I was rescued. I'll keep trying."

Mason's eyes softened as he looked at me.

I retold the story of meeting Brandon the next day without coming up with any new revelations.

"One last question." Mason was almost being conversational now. "When you arrived at the back of the building on the day of the fire, did you see Rico and Isabella Bruno?"

"I don't know, I could have, there was so much going on." I tried to picture it. "Wait. I do remember hearing my name and seeing both of them huddled together on the sidewalk. Yes, I definitely did." *Whew, I'm proud of myself.*

"Was there anything about how they looked or what they were wearing that indicated that they had been back inside the pizza parlor after returning from your block party? Aprons? Cooking utensils in their hands?"

Just when I thought that Mason was turning nice, he throws me this curve ball.

"I don't know, it all happened in seconds, and as soon as Bardot took off that was all I focused on."

I felt ashamed. I'd let Rico and Isabella down by not being able to provide them with an airtight alibi. But this was serious stuff; it wasn't like manipulating Augie into seeing our side of an event.

Mason thanked me for my time, and I believed that he meant it. My fire boys walked me out and we promised to meet up again soon.

Public service is indeed a noble profession, and we need to treat its servants accordingly.

Chapter Eight

The next day our second emergency Wine Club of the week was scheduled, and it was my turn to host. The fall weather (even though it was still seventy-six degrees outside) got me inspired to bake. When I lived in New York, baking was a big pastime of mine, especially when it was nasty outside and you just couldn't afford to go out to eat more than once or twice a month.

What? You think that I should just eat salads day in and day out? Have you met me?

I had most of the ingredients I needed but lacked two key components—really good English butter and fresh plums. You see I'd decided to make a plum cheesecake with a pistachio, shortbread crust, so I headed out to Whole Foods. I only shop there for specialty items because it is crazy to pay twenty-three dollars for soy sauce at "Whole Paycheck" as they call it.

So you can imagine my surprise when I walked in and saw Marisol talking to Julia Roberts. It is not unusual to see celebrities in the stores around here, but seeing Marisol conversing with one like they are best buds was a new one on me.

Just then I felt my phone vibrate in my purse. I took it out and saw that Liza Gilhooly was calling. I knew she had a busy schedule, and if I didn't pick up, I may not connect with her again all day. But I also was desperate to find out what Marisol had to talk about with an Oscar-winning actress. My sleuth sense got the better of me.

"Hi, Liza, you survived your night of property showings?"

"Hah, yes I did, and let's just say there were some interesting developments."

I was getting the sense that Liza was a late-stage cougar.

"I'd love to hear all about it, but I'm in Whole Foods right now and I really don't want to add to the people that are always on their phones in here talking loudly about their self-importance."

Her now trademark Liza laugh vibrated off my eardrum.

"Okay I'll make it quick, and I'm not sure how much help this is, but I remembered one of the investors' first names. It only came to me because it was somewhat unusual."

"Great, what was it?"

"Valentin. I remember asking him if he'd be my valentine, but I don't think that he appreciated the ribbing. This guy didn't have much of a sense of humor. I got no last name though; I'm not even sure if I was ever told it."

"Can you describe what he looked like? Age, ethnicity?"

"That's what's kooky . . . he was in his car and had a driver. A black Mercedes. He was in the backseat and had lowered his window a tad. He was wearing dark Wayfarer sunglasses, so he really could have looked like anyone."

I spotted Marisol again . . . this time sweeping through the nuts and grains aisle with her shopping cart. "You've been a terrific help, Liza, more than you know. Thank you!"

"Take care, toots." And Liza ended the call.

"Looking for something to make yourself more regular, Marisol?" I asked after catching up with her.

"I don't know what you're talking about. I came here looking for spiced watermelon rinds and cola syrup in case I get an upset stomach."

"Good thinking because once you eat those watermelon rinds, you're going to need a remedy."

"Oh, and you owe me big time," she said as she opened the lid of one of the bins that line the aisle with fruits and nuts, and plucked out a dried apricot.

"You better pay for that or I'll tell the manager. And just what were you and Julia Roberts jawing about?"

"Who? I wasn't talking to nobody."

"Come on I saw you, and it's hard to mistake someone that I've seen in all her movies at least twice."

Marisol ignored me and diverted her attention to the selection of infused honey products. I hated when she did that almost as much as I hated when she paid attention to me.

"I hope you paid off your credit cards this month, Halsey, because you're going to be buying me a lot of stuff in here."

"The hell I am, but I'll help you look for something to cure your insanity. Where is the witches' section?" I said, looking around.

"Fine, then I won't tell you what I found out."

She had me. In a moment of desperation yesterday, I'd asked Marisol to try and worm out some information about the owners of the burned strip mall from Augie—naturally without mentioning me.

"You've talked to Augie, haven't you?"

Marisol clammed up.

"What's your favorite cut of beef again, Marisol? Let's head to the butcher and I'll treat you to a nice steak dinner."

"I want lobster."

"The seafood section it is."

Marisol was disappointed when she learned that Whole Foods didn't have a tank with live lobsters. I suspect that she'd had plans of taking one home, putting a leash on it, and going for a walk together down Rose Avenue. She settled for two tails, some jumbo shrimp, and herbed butter.

"Okay, you happy? Tell me what Augie said."

Still the silent treatment.

"What now?"

"I gotta wash this down with something."

My mind immediately went to boric acid. Is that bad of me?

"Wine or beer?"

"I dunno, I gotta see."

"Okay, while you see, did Augie give you a name or not? Who owns that strip mall?"

We were now in the wine section, and I could tell that Marisol had no idea what she was looking at. While she is an honorary member of the Rose Avenue Wine Club, I suspect that she subscribes more to the "Wine is fine but liquor is quicker" adage. When I noticed her focusing on the price tags, I was onto her.

"You know, all the famous seafood celebrities drink beer with a meal like this. Shall we take a gander?"

I steered her over to the refrigerated case just in time as she was reaching for a limited edition bottle of Veuve Clicquot.

"Maybe I want margaritas."

"They don't sell that here. What did Augie say?"

"He doesn't have a name."

"What? Have you just been yanking my chain?"

"But he has an address."

I wanted to shove her in the case and hang an ON SALE sign in the window.

"Okay, I'll take those Coronas."

I stopped her from opening the glass door.

"Address first."

"I could call Security."

"Great. I need to tell them about that dried apricot you shoplifted."

Marisol reached into her giant purse, which I was convinced led all the way to Alice in Wonderland's mad tea party.

"Here."

She handed me a scrap of paper with her chicken scratch handwriting on it. I made sure that it was legible.

"Maybe you want some limes to go with your beer, Marisol."

"No, I want spiced watermelon rinds."

"Who on earth got you into those?"

"Julia Roberts."

Wine Club convened a little late that afternoon; it seemed that everyone was juggling busy schedules. Sally was the first to arrive, and upon smelling the sweet, nutty aroma in the air declared, "You've been baking, bless your sugar honey heart! I should have worn sweatpants."

"Hi, girlfriend, plum cheesecake. It's resting in the oven with the door ajar, so don't you go nosing around in there or you'll crack it. I need fifteen more minutes."

Once Sally had opened my door and the odor of baked goods had wafted down the street, the rest of the girls arrived in fast succession. When Aimee brought up the rear, I moved to close the door but felt some resistance. I looked through one of the three windows in the top third of my oak front door but couldn't see anybody. Thinking that it was the wind I tried again, and this time got some stronger push back. I watched Marisol squeeze in and march over to one of the living room sofas.

"Since when do you come to Wine Club, Marisol?" My tone was less than welcoming.

"I'm a member, I brought my flask," she said, dangling the miniature item and its keychain from her little finger.

A couple years back when we'd solved our first murder mystery, Marisol had been instrumental in its success. It was the holidays, we were at Sally and Joe's celebrating and drinking lots of wine, and not thinking about the repercussions—we extended an invitation for Marisol to become a member of the Rose Avenue Wine Club. Now the only time she shows up is if she wants something. Today I'm guessing it's cheesecake.

Aimee had offered to provide the wine today, and when I told her that I was serving dessert, she went out and got a few bottles of Lune d'Argent White Bordeaux blend. Perfect.

"If I'd known that we were doing sweet stuff, I would have brought my Jordan almonds," Peggy observed, settling in.

We could have sat outside, but I was doing my best to pretend that it was a cool and crisp autumn and that as the sun began to set, we might think about lighting the fireplace.

"Penelope's busy at the winery with the kitchen build-out, but she promised to call in," I told the group.

The winery was named for Abigail Rose, Malcolm's great-grandmother. Malcolm had been orphaned at a young age, and as he grew up outside of San Francisco he became transfixed with tracing his familial roots. After much research and legwork, he discovered that Abigail Rose lived in the Los Angeles area, on Rose Avenue in fact. Unfortunately, she passed soon after they reconnected but left behind an estate that afforded him the means to purchase the vineyard. The overnight visit was going to be the high point in the fall for the Rose Avenue Wine Club.

When Aimee had filled each of our glasses, we paused with reverence for a toast. For us it was like hearing the national anthem before the game began. With that behind us, I served everyone cheesecake, which brought renewed silence and introspection.

"Do I taste pistachios?" Sally asked, breaking apart a bit of crust and searching for green meats.

I nodded.

"I can tell that it had plums because you've put some halves on the top," Peggy noted.

"There's something else, a tang that pulls it all together. We spent an entire week on this when I was in pastry school. It counterbalances the sweetness of the shortbread and cream. What is it, Halsey?" Aimee looked frustrated that she hadn't deciphered the entire recipe.

"You all give up?"

Nods all around.

"Ginger root juice."

"Praise the Lord, my achy muscles thank you." Sally's latest armchair study project was on the health benefits of spices around the world.

"Will this help my arthritis?"

"Peggy, any minute now you'll be saying 'what arthritis?'"

"I'll take another slice of ginger and don't be so skimpy this time."

I glared at Marisol.

My cell phone rang and I saw that it was Penelope, so I put her on speaker.

"Hellooo, ladies, and what delectables are being served for today's event?"

We played "show and tell" for her.

"Lovely. Things are progressing here as far as the kitchen goes, and as for the harvest . . . I'm trying to stay out of the way, but I hear Malcolm and Andrew arguing all the time. I'm keeping my fingers crossed. I'll have to get back to work shortly because I don't want them to think that I'm slacking off."

"Then we need to get right to our updates on the fire."

Aimee waved her hand, hoping that I'd call on her. I nodded.

"This is Aimee, Penelope," she said in her auditorium voice. "Can you hear me?"

We all moved about a foot back from her.

"Crystal clear, Aimee. You mustn't shout."

"Okay. So I talked to my landlord for the yogurt shop, Mr. Babayan. He only knows about the guys that own the strip mall by reputation, and he says to steer clear of them or they'll 'curse your kefir.'" She tried to imitate an Armenian accent. "I know it sounds funny, but when he said it I was sure scared."

Marisol and I exchanged glances.

"Then I suggest that we take a guarded approach," Sally announced.

"What the hell does that mean?" I poured Peggy more wine because she was getting impatient and cranky.

"It means that we should take guards with us for protection when approaching them." Sally gave Peggy the "stink eye."

"I was able to slip Brandon's name into the conversation at supper last night," Penelope jumped in. "I said that Halsey and he were acquaintances and wasn't it such a small world. Andrew got really interested in hearing more about you, Halsey, which is odd since he knows very well that you and Jack are planning your wedding at Abigail Rose Winery. Which reminds me, are you two lovebirds coming up tomorrow?"

I'd almost forgotten. I really need to get my head into these nuptials. "We'll be there. Around two, correct?"

"Perfect. Oh, and Andrew didn't have too terribly much to report on Brandon, just that he had big dreams. Sounded a bit odd to me . . . I'm going to ring off, ladies. Cheers!"

"Bye, Penelope," we all chimed in.

"I didn't want to risk having Penelope betray a confidence to Andrew, so now that she's gone I have one more important piece of news on this case."

"Spit it out, girl!" Peggy shouted, and Marisol slowly released some cheesecake from her mouth.

"Okay, Peggy, you all remember Jack's friend Mark who is with the DEA?" I had their attention. "It seems that there was a safe in the drugstore that disappeared after the fire, and it contained mostly opioid drugs for special prescriptions. It was there before the fire but not after, and it was built to withstand a very hot fire."

"Well that sweetens the pot. Do you think that somehow Andrew is mixed up in this, Halsey?"

"I have no reason to, but until we know how close a friendship he has with Brandon I figured that it was better to be safe than sorry."

"Good thinking, girl." Sally took her plate to the kitchen. I know how much she loves my cheesecake, so I'm betting that without a plate she would be less tempted to go for a second slice. My galley kitchen was small but very serviceable to me. It had an old, glass electric stove top that worked really well, and the best news was that I had a double oven. Neither was terribly large, but each had its own temperature settings, and especially around Thanksgiving it was perfect for cooking a bird on top and keeping the sides warm below.

"These things are boring. I'm going to watch baseball," Marisol announced, leaving.

"I should head out too . . . you've inspired me to try out some new baking recipes, Halsey." Aimee stood and made an unselfconscious big stretch that separated her tank top from her leggings, exposing a pleasingly plump belly. Aimee loved food and she loved consuming it.

"Thanks for the wine, Aimee."

Peggy started to stand, but I put my hand on her arm.

"Looks like there's enough for two more glasses, Peggy." I held the bottle up to the light.

She acquiesced and we waited for the front door to close.

I was about to clue her in on the address that Marisol had given me for the strip mall owners but wanted to clear something up first. "You seem a little uptight today, Peggy. Is everything okay? You and Charlie getting along?"

"We're fine, everything's fine."

I looked at her.

"Really. Just the little aches and pains of a woman of my age in the colder months."

Peggy never talked about getting old, so it made my stomach sink. "You'd tell us if it was anything serious, right?"

"Of course I would. Don't you have a wedding to plan?" She said this with a smile and gave me a hug before leaving.

I couldn't help but wonder if Peggy was telling me the truth.

Chapter Nine

The drive up the Pacific Coast Highway on this glorious late September Saturday was indeed a slice of heaven. Overnight a cool front had moved in dropping the temperature to the high sixties and giving me an excuse to wear long sleeves. I opted for a black and white French sailor shirt, black Capris, and white sneaks.

Jaunty but refined.

Jack and I were headed to the Abigail Rose Winery to talk to Malcolm and Penelope about hosting our wedding there. They categorically refused to let us pay for anything beyond out-of-pocket expenses, which doesn't set well with either of us.

But I am working on a robust website for them with everything from venue videos to special events to wine ordering and real-time inventory tracking. Jack has a very special surprise for Malcolm and Penelope—one he had been working on for five weeks.

This union that I'd been evading for almost three years was finally on its way to becoming a reality. I should explain. My foot dragging has nothing to do with Jack. I love him deeply and I couldn't ask for a better guy. He is kind, funny, smart, cute as hell, and sexy. It is the marriage part that I continue to have trouble with.

You see this will be my second time around. The first happened when I was way too young, and I naively fell in love with love rather than the man. I think that I knew during the honeymoon that the marriage wasn't going to work, but I hate being a quitter. So instead I kept trying to fix the marriage, which in New York City is quite the challenge. You can't just buy him a new grill and an apron with THE BIGGEST WIENER IS NOT ON THE BBQ printed on it. We didn't have the money to redo the apartment to "our taste." But mostly I wanted to work on making a life for us while he was perfectly happy with his own life just the way it was. Don't get me wrong, when I realized that this was like watering a dead plant, I showed my displeasure in distinctly Halsey ways. I'd been to an all girls' Catholic high school and had learned from the best of them.

One week after being on the receiving end of constant criticism from him, I had a big box of Krispy Kremes sent to his Friday creative meeting. I knew that he'd show off how much he was loved to the group. On the inside lid of the box I had written in big letters YOU DO *NOT* COMPLETE ME. And I'd taken one bite out of each of the dozen donuts. Soon after I was "Halsey, the young divorcée."

I knew that this time around it was totally different, but to quote Wham! In "Last Christmas," I was "once bitten and twice shy."

I looked over at my amber-eyed redwood of a man and saw that he was grinning from ear to ear while he drove. That made me smile. I saw his right eye move ever so slightly in my direction.

"One, two, or three?" he asked me.

The sound of his voice sent Bardot into an excited whine. We were in Jack's massive truck that had crates in the back to transport dogs. In addition to Bardot, Clarence—his giant schnauzer—was also along for a day in the country.

"Don't make me come back there," I yelled, which only escalated my dog's vocal emissions.

"Psst," Jack said softly, and silence was restored to the vehicle.

"How do you do that?"

"You have to answer my question first: one, two, or three?"

"One, two, or three what, Jack?"

"Kids!"

I groaned.

"You are aware that I turned thirty-eight this year?"

"Then we'd better get crackin'."

"Dear God," I said, but deep down the thought gave me a warm feeling.

When we turned off PCH, the din of traffic disappeared and we were moving in the midst of a wooded, verdant hillside and valley. The road up the hill was crudely paved but organic to the surrounding atmosphere that included a man-made stone wall that lined the twists and turns that led us to Abigail Rose Winery.

Of course we'd been here for Malcolm and Penelope's wedding, but there was so much going on that day I'm afraid that the details and nuances of the spectacular location have been lost from my memory.

"Can you slow down, Jack?"

"You're not squeamish around switchbacks, are you?"

"No, I want to breathe in this gorgeous scenery, including you on a leisurely drive."

That got him and we slowed down, and he opened all the windows so the sweet air could waft through the moving vehicle. Around us on all sides were rows and rows of green-leafed grapevines, and I wondered where another vineyard ended and Malcolm and Penelope's began. Since the grapes were planted on stepped hillsides, I can only imagine the backbreaking work that was required all through the growing process. Penelope had mentioned that they were bringing in some thirty day-laborers for the harvest.

When this hill crested to a flat drive the winery came into view, and we pulled into a gravel lot and parked under the cool shade of a massive oak tree. I got out and wished that we had taken my car instead of Jack's conspicuous truck, but we had precious cargo on board.

Jack got out on his side, and we heard a cooing sound coming from the main entrance that overlooked the valley all the way down to Malibu Lake.

"You're here . . . welcome!" Penelope said, coming down the steps from the large, arched heavy-wooded door to the winery.

"Hello to you," I said, embracing her. Jack joined in on the hug.

"Malcolm will be by presently. He's just washing up from inspecting the fields. Shall we have a glass of wine on the patio, yes? It won't be too cold for you?"

"You guys are such weather wimps." Jack laughed.

"Come, we've mended this stone patio to the side here and set out some mission tables and chairs. I've got a claret that I'd love for you to sample."

"Is it okay if I let the dogs out to ramble around? Clarence will make sure that Bardot sticks to one bunch of grapes, I promise."

"Of course, Jack, this place is heaven for dogs."

Jack and I smiled at each other. We watched him open the big double doors at the back of his truck and then the doors to two heavy-duty crates that the dogs ride in for safety. Clarence, the giant schnauzer, appeared first, hopped down, and sat at attention watching for Jack to give further direction. Bardot took a flying leap out, raced around, sniffed, peed, and then joined Clarence in a sit/stay.

I'd give her a C+ for execution and an A for creativity.

"Who let the dogs out? Woof, woof, woof, woof." Malcolm sauntered out, gave Penelope and then me a peck on the cheek, and settled at the patio table.

I never thought I'd see the day when Malcolm was singing, let alone Bahamian Junkanoo.

We watched Jack release the hounds from their sitting stance. Bardot was the first to sprint off around the flat top mesa above the hillside of grapevines. Graceful and elegant, Clarence followed, his long legs helping him catch up to her quickly. They played a little "stop and dodge," marked the same spot one after the other, and scampered down the hill.

Jack returned to the table. He'd left the back door to the truck open to air it out. As he sat down we heard a soft whimper.

"So this is the claret we've been hearing about all

summer." Jack took a long sniff and then rolled a sip around in his mouth.

"Claret is a British term used, unofficially, in reference to red Bordeaux wine. I decided to try this in honor of my English rose, Penelope. The red wines of Bordeaux are blends, mostly based on cabernet sauvignon and merlot," Malcolm explained.

"Wait, so the grapes that went into this came from France?" I was confused.

"No, love, they were grown right here."

She held up her glass to the sunlight, making the deep red liquid a slight bit transparent, and swirled the elixir gently in her glass.

Malcolm helped Penelope out. "Technically this has been made in the style of Bordeaux, meaning that we used a blend of Cabernet, Malbec, and Syrah grapes. We made a small batch with the grapes that were here when we purchased the winery, but this year will be our first full harvest. We'll be able to offer Cabs, Malbec, and of course, more of this." Malcolm raised his glass in another toast.

"If you've ever watched *Downton Abbey*, you'd notice that us Brits have a long history of calling anything red 'claret.'"

"Whatever you call it, this is absolutely delicious!" I declared, and Jack nodded effusively.

"Thank you . . . that's a relief to hear. We're still bottling the rest of this harvest to make room for the new one. They love the wine," Malcolm shouted to Andrew as he appeared on the patio.

"How much did you ply them with before they said that?" Andrew asked, shaking Jack's hand and then leaning in to give me a peck on the cheek. He sat down and poured himself a glass.

We've barely met . . .

"No, really, you guys have a winner here." *I've never seen Jack happier.*

"Halsey, have you had a tour of the vineyards since you were last here? Well over a year ago according to Malcolm." Andrew stood up ready to whisk me away.

"Maybe later we can all go, Andrew," Penelope said with a bit of a hard edge to her voice. "Jack and Halsey are here to plan their wedding with us."

Andrew looked from her to me, and I tilted my engagement ring until it caught the sun and set off a nova-size starburst.

"Yes, of course. Just let me know when. Do I hear some animal crying?"

Jack looked at me and I nodded.

"Yes, you do, and it is coming from my truck. Excuse me, I'll be right back."

Penelope looked at me, smiled, and shrugged her shoulders in anticipation. I took a minute to drink in my beautiful surroundings. A light breeze wafted over us coming from the ocean. The winery main house sat atop a medium-size hill and looked out in all directions to similar vineyards of varying heights and expanses. It was like looking at undulating corduroy with soft green ribs. I was both relaxed and excited at the thought of saying our "I dos" here.

"You're going to let us see the creature, aren't you, Jack?" she called out.

"Even better, Penelope, I'm going to let you hold her."

Jack reappeared from inside the back of the truck carrying a black ball of fluff.

"Wow," Malcolm exclaimed.

"What is this adorable little beast and what is his

or"—Penelope paused for further inspection—
"her name?"

"That's for you two to decide. Jack wanted to show you how much we appreciate being able to hold our wedding here, and he's been saying from day one that you need a dog or three to protect the winery."

The pup took instantly to Penelope and began licking her and whimpering. That sent Bardot and Clarence racing back to us.

"As you can see, I have worked with giant schnauzers a lot."

"Jack, are you saying that this little thing is going to turn into that?"

"Precisely, Malcolm, maybe even bigger. Psst," Jack uttered, and Bardot and Clarence lay down quietly. "This breed was developed in Germany to drive cattle and later to serve as guard dogs at the breweries. They went on to become excellent trained police dogs but didn't catch on in the States because we had already adopted the German shepherd."

They all stared in awe at Jack. I noticed that Bardot, try as she might, was getting distracted by something in the air.

"What Jack hasn't told you is that he's spent the past five weeks working with her, teaching her the basic commands and more, housebreaking her and getting all her puppy vet procedures done."

"I'll be coming back to keep working with her and more importantly with you all to make this an awesome relationship. She's already a fabulous dog."

I was so proud of Jack.

With all this going on I almost didn't notice Bardot sneak out of position and circle around the back of us on the patio.

"This is so cool, a far cry from that mutt that lived with us when we were kids . . . what was his name, Malc?"

Malcolm looked at Andrew and I could see that they were both trying to remember.

"Was it Roni? Like Rice-a-Roni?" Malcolm asked.

"That's it." Andrew clapped his hands loudly.

That attracted Bardot's attention and she raced over to him for some exploratory sniffing.

"The obvious thing to name her would be Rose," Penelope said, letting Malcolm have a chance at some sloppy kiss bonding.

"How about Malibu Rose?" Malcolm suggested, giggling at the dog's attention.

"Perfect!" I said after seeing that Penelope agreed.

"Hey, you're going to need to buy me dinner before you continue doing that," Andrew said to Bardot, only half joking.

Bardot had her nose buried halfway up Andrew's jeans leg. I'd never seen her act this badly, and I wondered if the presence and all the attention on the new puppy had made her jealous.

"Bardot," Jack said calmly but when she didn't stop, he gave her a more forceful "PSST!"

She finally came up for air. But not before she had thoroughly embarrassed Jack and myself.

Chapter Ten

I dreamed of long dresses and bountiful bouquets of flowers, letting the most perfect wedding scenario play out in my mind. In the dream even Bardot was on her best behavior.

We slept in late Sunday morning and after some coffee and eggs, Jack suggested that we take the dogs up to the CARA testing area for some drills. I could have gone right back to bed and watched the *Halloween* marathon on TV, but I thought again about Bardot's strange behavior and figured that this would be a good chance to set her straight—that I'm boss.

Who am I kidding?

CARA had access to some ten acres of land in the Santa Monica Mountains for training dog/handler teams so that the pair can ultimately pass their certification to become accredited rescue teams. I'd watched Jack conduct exercises often up here and still marvel at the way he can work with dogs and how well both parties in a team can be trained. It is a noble service, but, as smart as Bardot is, I'm afraid that we will never make it to the major leagues. Jack doesn't believe that . . . he knows what Bardot can do. Which leaves us with who is really dragging down the team: *me*. It seems that I can only be trained so much, which is fine with me.

"Let's work with Bardot on a long leash for a while," Jack suggested after we'd unloaded some gear. "This is perfect because there are lots of other distractions around her—dogs, people, and toys. It's your job to keep her totally focused on you, Halsey."

I nodded, albeit halfheartedly.

"Let's try with a Frisbee. Toss it just as far as the leash reaches, and then have her get it and bring it back to you."

Bardot sat at my feet staring at the orange disk and me. I swear that the corner of one eye had been pulled toward a squirrel that was running back into the woods with somebody's sandwich. I wasn't sure which one interested her more. The only thing that I knew for sure was that Bardot thought that Frisbee was a pedestrian sport better suited to border collies.

"Here's the deal, Bardot," I whispered to her. "You pretend that you're really interested in retrieving this toy when I toss it, bring it back to me, and turn and smile at Jack. Got it? You do that and I'll let you sleep under the covers tonight."

I tossed the Frisbee.

"Go get it, Bardot!" I said with feigned excitement. Nothing.

"There it is, there's your toy!"

"One of the other dogs is going to take it!"

Bardot lifted up her paw and examined a nail.

"Fine, you're being a brat."

Jack was laughing. "Halsey, you can't run out of patience or you've lost the battle."

"She's not a 'jump in the air and grab a piece of

round plastic' kind of girl. She's more of a 'take me to a crime scene and let's catch baddies' motivated dog."

"Like mother, like daughter." Jack came over to us and we all plopped down on the grass.

"Yesterday got me excited to plan our wedding, how about you?"

Jack perked up at hearing this. Given my fickle attitude to the entire institution, I suspect that he's always prepared to hear the worst from me.

"That's great, babe. But maybe we should consider having it on a beach somewhere, maybe the Kona coast in Hawaii."

"A destination wedding? Wow, that came out of nowhere."

"Just a suggestion, and we'd already be there for our honeymoon."

I studied Jack. He wasn't looking at me and he was tugging on the side of his beard. This was a telltale sign that he was worried about something.

"Okay, buster, spill it. What's really bothering you about having the wedding at the winery? I think that between the website I'm doing and the wonderful dog you just gave them that we come out sort of even with investment of our time."

"It's not that, Halsey, and you know I love it up there."

"Then what? You getting cold feet, Jack?"

"No! God no!"

"Then tell me."

My cell phone rang and I saw that it was Sally calling. "Hi, honey, what's up?"

"You sound like you're outside, where are you?"

"Jack and I are at the CARA training area, running with Bardot." I looked over and both Jack and Bardot were now stretched out on their backs soaking up some sun.

"Well, you might want to get back here. I just ran into Isabella. I was driving past the strip mall on my way to my CPR class when I saw Augie get out of his car. A police cruiser pulled up behind him. Naturally, I turned onto the side street and got out to see what the fuss was about. All three of the men went into the burned-out entry to the pizza joint, and when they returned they had Rico in cuffs and drove away with him. Then Isabella came out and she was in hysterics."

"Oh no!"

Both Jack and Bardot sat up.

"What did she say? Did Augie explain why he arrested Rico?"

"He was his usual evasive self. Said that they just had some questions for him."

"Crap, we're heading out now. Meet you at your house, and you may want to assemble the Wine Club."

"Will do, and I have Isabella with me."

"I'll start the truck," Jack said, moving into action.

"Wait one minute. You were going to tell me why you were having second thoughts about a Malibu vineyard wedding."

"It was nothing . . . I'm totally over it. We'd better scoot."

I doubt that it was nothing.

The girls were all assembled by the time we arrived. We met in Sally's beautiful backyard haven around her pool and spa. If my backyard looked like the Tiki Taki Hotel, then Sally's resembled a Costa Rican rain forest. Dream catchers hung from old tree limbs, water ran in the Koi pond at the back corner, and tribal masks and iron statues of stylized Africans gave the feel of being in an entirely other world.

Sally's husband Joe and her cousin Jimmy were watching football, and Jack jumped at the opportunity to join them. I couldn't blame him.

"I got here as fast as I could. What's the latest? Has anyone talked to Augie?"

I settled into the last remaining unoccupied patio chair and was handed a glass of chardonnay.

"Nothing yet," Peggy replied. "But it's Sunday and he may have to wait for his boss to get into the station."

"Isabella, I'm so sorry. I know that you've already done this, but would you mind repeating for me exactly what happened?"

"Sure, Halsey." She was trying to pull herself together.

"Rico and I were at the site making sure that there was nothing left to salvage. The insurance adjuster had been there on Saturday and I wanted to double-check everything before he issued his report. Just in case they decided to go light on the claim as Rico says it."

"Smart."

"Then Detective Augie called Rico and asked where he was. Rico told him and Augie said that he'd be right over."

"That's about when I was driving by," Sally told the group.

"This is all so horrible, it makes me sick." Aimee was both teary and huffy. "They can't just go arresting people for no reason. Can they, Peggy?"

"Of course not . . . what a load of rotten applesauce."

I noticed that Isabella had a strange look on her face.

"Did Augie give you both any reason for why he was taking Rico in?"

"He may have said something about a safe."

"What about the safe, Isabella?"

"I guess that the cops found one in an alley about six blocks away. It had been broken open."

"What in the sand dabs from Chez Jay's does that have to do with Rico?" Sally shouted. Chez Jay's was one of her favorite old restaurants on Ocean Avenue directly across from the Santa Monica Pier.

"I don't like this. I know this is going to be bad," said Aimee, the harbinger of doom.

"Please go on, Isabella." I tried to be soothing.

"Next to it they found a piece of metal. At first they didn't know what it was, but they later figured out that it was part of a dough hook." Isabella looked down to the ground in shame.

"Again, so what?" Peggy crossed her arms in defiance.

"It is the same kind of hook Rico uses. Used. That's why they took Rico, to get his fingerprints. He's the only one that works that big mixer machine. Me, I'm scared of it."

There it was, a hole so deep that you'd need a hundred-foot ladder to get out of.

I had no doubt that they'd find a match between Rico's prints and those on the hook.

It was time to get the cops looking in another direction, and I had an address that might just be the distraction we need.

"Ladies, I have a new mission for us."

Chapter Eleven

Monday morning right at ten I waited for Liza Gilhooly outside her locked office door. I was starting to get the message that punctuality was not Liza's strong suit. I walked around the back of the small office building, where I assumed that there were parking spaces available for the tenants.

Moments later a Pepto-Bismol-pink Cadillac Eldorado pulled into the lot. I fully expected to hear "Freeway of Love" blaring from the car's old speakers. Instead I saw Liza driving this boat with one hand, while deep in conversation on the phone she was holding in her other hand. I made a mental note to steer clear of all fuchsia-colored vehicles that I spotted on the road.

She remained on the phone long after she'd shut off the engine, and I wondered if I should go back around to the front. This Liza Gilhooly was certainly an odd one, even to me. She looked up and seemed to notice me for the first time and quickly ended the call.

"Sorry, Halsey, I was talking to my brother and couldn't get him to hang up. You know how siblings can be." She gave out a trademark Liza laugh as she swung open the large and heavy pink door of her automobile.

I could have sworn that she told me she was an only child. What an odd thing to lie about. And why?

"Come on, honey . . . let's go inside and I'll put on some water for tea."

I took Liza through the schematic for her website and she had few changes or comments. In fact, I doubted if she was giving me more than fifty percent of her attention.

"So the next step is for me to frame the technical aspects of the functionality and then start working on the look and feel. Is this the logo that you want me to use?" I held up one of her business cards.

"No! I mean I'm having someone work on a new one. Can we just put in something generic for now, like a drawing of an office building?"

"Sure, no problem," I said, wondering why she'd had such a strong reaction. "I literally don't need the artwork until just before we go live."

"Okay good. Listen, I'm going to be jammed for the next few weeks, so I'll probably be out of touch. If you need something from me just send a text and I'll try and get to it."

It was clear that, however nicely, I was getting the bum's rush.

She must have noticed what she was doing.

"Thanks, honey. You do great work, Halsey. I'm excited about my website."

"You're welcome. I'm pretty self-sufficient, and so I'll just keep going on this until I need content from you. Don't work too hard."

She gave me a warm smile, and I decided to head out the front this time.

"One more thing, Liza. Have you thought any more about this Valentin guy who may own the strip mall? Any last names come to mind?"

"Yes, I did think about it, Halsey."

My spirits lifted.

"I realized that I got mixed up. Valentin was the name of an accountant I had years ago. I never knew the building owners' names."

"Okay, it was worth a try."

"Toodles, toots."

She closed the front door, and I heard the lock turn in its cylinder. I counted at least two and possibly four lies that she'd told me today: *Liza said she was talking to her brother, yet earlier she'd said she was an only child. I'm pretty sure that she was feigning her excitement for the website—she seemed bored and unfocused when I went over it with her. The bit about holding off on the logo was odd, and I've never heard of an accountant named Valentin.*

As Sally merged onto the 105 Freeway that cuts a path from the west to the east of Southern California, I insisted that we go over our plan once again for safe measure. I was riding shotgun and Peggy, Aimee, and Marisol were in the backseat. We'd tried to get away without Marisol but that, of course, was a fool's errand. When Sally pulled in my driveway to pick me up, Marisol slithered into the SUV faster than a buttered bullet.

"Aimee, today you are our star spy. You'll walk into Provident Commerce Group's office and announce that you're there for the job you saw posted on

Monster.com. Mention word processing and light filing."

"I don't know, Halsey."

"Come on, you're perfect for the role. If anyone tries to give you flack, you start crying and say that 'your babies won't have Christmas again.'"

"You don't think that's a little heavy-handed?" Sally was superstitious about using her favorite holiday in a scam.

"If these guys did burn down their own building with no concern of who was inside, then we're going to need something with lots of heartstring-pulling power to get through to them. You might want to add, Aimee, that you'll look in trash bins the day after Christmas for discarded broken toys to make do."

"I'm going to puke." Marisol looked disgusted.

"There are motion sickness bags back there," Sally quickly advised. "There's a box of two dozen tucked just under the driver's seat."

"I think that Marisol was speaking figuratively. We're getting closer. May I continue?"

"Of course, you can never go over the maneuvers for a mission too much." Peggy was in CIA mode.

"Okay, I'll be waiting outside their office in the hallway, waiting to snap photos of them undetected if they decide to slip out a side door to make a hasty retreat."

"And thanks to Google Maps we know that this building has an underground garage. Sally and I will start filming license plates the minute we arrive and then wait to see which car or cars they get into. One way or another we'll be able to identify them."

Marisol looked at Peggy with great admiration. In

her twisted world she saw herself as the second in command to the high priestess of spydom.

"What about me, what will I be doing?" Marisol posed this question to Peggy.

In unison we all said, "Waiting in the car!"

"We mean it, Marisol." I glared at her.

"Good luck with that," she whispered.

"If I have to tie you up I will."

"No, you won't."

"I will too."

"Quiet you two, there's the building. I'm going to drive around once so that we can get a good look at the entrances and exits. And get a feel for the place."

After we'd taken the Downey exit off the freeway, we wove our way to the unglamorous business district that was still within honking distance from the incessant noise of speeding traffic. The neighborhood looked iffy at best, and a part of me wanted to turn back and head to the safe bosom of Rose Avenue.

"Okay, I got it, the garage spills out onto that side street. We can park on the main drag just below it, Sally, so if for whatever reason we need to follow them we'll be in position."

"Got it, Peggy."

When the car was settled into its spot a silence fell over us. I felt a pang of guilt.

"You know, guys, we—"

The backseat door opened and before I could finish my thought, I saw Marisol scamper into the office building.

Aimee and I waved good-bye to Sally and Peggy and entered the building's lobby. The address Marisol had gotten from Augie didn't include a suite number, and if they were operating under a different business name in here, then we were pretty much out of luck. The building roster displayed some forty offices or so. My eyes went to the P's and ran down the list until I saw the words PROVIDENT, SUITE 311.

We decided to take the stairs more to try and steady our nerves than for any other reason. When we reached the landing of the third level, we stopped and took a breath.

"You can still back out, Aimee, if you want to."

"And let down Rico and Isabella and all of you girls? Hell no . . . what's the worst that can happen?"

I wished she hadn't asked that.

"Okay, but remember that if you sense any trouble just punch the fire alarm app that I put on your phone. It's so loud that they won't know where it's coming from. Then head for the door and I'll be waiting. Okay?"

"Okay, let's nail these flunkers!"

Wow, Aimee had channeled her "take no prisoners, dog with a bone" resolve.

We went through the stairwell door and into the hallway. It was pretty typical looking for seventies' office décor. The carpet looked original as did the stains. Striped beige wallpaper had faded from the sun in the spots where tiny windows let in light. In those areas it looked like the walls were weeping. We walked along until we saw the doorplate of 311. There was no company name visible.

We exchanged thumbs up, and I slid around the corner and located the second door to the suite. A little spittle of bile came up and burned the back of my throat.

I heard Aimee knock on the door and then immediately walk in.

The sounds of muffled voices came from behind the side door almost immediately. I was pretty sure that they came from men, but I couldn't make out anything that they were saying. Then came the wails of someone sobbing. Was Aimee acting? Or was she really in distress.

"What's happening?" I heard behind me, and I must have jumped three feet.

The voice had come from someone pushing a janitorial caddy containing an industrial trash receptacle and slots for mops, brooms, cleaning supplies, and CAUTION WET FLOOR cones. All of these supplies camouflaged the person pushing the cart. Just then I could hear another round of sobbing and shouting.

"That doesn't sound good . . . hop in."

I peered around the caddy and sure enough there was Marisol dressed in a blue custodian smock and bandanna tied around her head.

"What the hell? That's trash; I'm not getting in there." I took one sniff of the big plastic bin and stepped back.

"Suit yourself. I'm going in."

Marisol thrust her weight onto the caddy and it lunged forward.

Crap, crap, crap.

"Wait! I can't believe I'm doing this," I whispered, grabbing both sides of the reinforced rubber trash bin to lower myself in.

"Got to cover you up," I heard Marisol say, and then felt a pile of garbage including the wet remains of a drinking cup splash over me.

"I hate you."

"Shut up. We're going in."

I felt the cart roll and heard a door open.

"We didn't call for the janitor. We're working here!" It was a man's voice spoken with an accent that I couldn't quite place.

"Up to you. I got to finish my shift early today on account of bunion surgery. At least it's covered by workman's comp. You don't want me to clean, then you'll be looking at this same mess all day tomorrow."

I gotta admit, Marisol's good.

"This place is a goddamn zoo today!" A different voice, also male. "You," he continued, "I promise you that we never posted any ads anywhere. Tell me who sent you and what you are doing here."

He must be talking to Aimee.

"I swear, it said that Providence Commerce Group was looking for help with word processing. Since I live five minutes away, I thought that this would be perfect for me. I could even go home at lunch and get the prep done for dinner."

"Ha hah!" I heard Marisol cackle.

Kill me now.

"This your business card, mister?"

"How'd you get that?"

"You got 'em out in this holder here. I assume this is a help yourself situation."

There was an exchange between the men in a language I didn't recognize.

"I ain't got no BM degree or nothing," Marisol continued. "But this card says PROVIDENT COMMERCE GROUP."

"So?"

"So the lady said 'Providence'; that's a horse of a different color. Whatever, I'm not going to keep standing here yapping with you, my feet are killing me. Have a nice day."

"I guess I made a mistake," I heard Aimee say as I felt the caddy move again.

"Val, let's get out of here. Now." The man's voice again.

When I heard the door close, I figured that we were back in the hallway.

"We'd better split too Marisol, before they figure out that we were lying."

"Good idea. Let's take the stairs."

I heard running and then it stopped.

"You coming, Halsey?"

"I really hate you, Marisol," I said, pushing myself up from under a blanket of trash.

Chapter Twelve

"What do you mean 'you can't be sure which car they drove off in'?"

"Just that. Four people got off the elevator, and we followed the wrong two." Peggy was frustrated and almost spat her words.

"Were they all men?" Aimee asked, gripping the arm rest as Sally merged back onto the freeway.

"Yes," Sally said.

"Just how do you know that these weren't our guys?" It was starting to sink into me that this could have all been a waste of time.

"We figured it out when they got into a truck with a JESUS EXTERMINATION sign on it and we heard one guy ask the other if he had the estimate forms."

"Maybe they were exorcists," Marisol muttered.

She really is nuts. Funny, but loca.

"Rats, well that eliminates one license plate from the film you took. How many cars were down there?"

"At least a dozen. I'm so sorry we let you down, Halsey." Sally sighed. "I'm afraid that we aren't even good enough for state work."

Wait, what now?

"Oh, we're going to come through. I've already sent the images to a friend of mine from back in the day."

Peggy means the CIA.

"He'll get me the names of the owners of all the cars we saw."

"Okay, good. Did I hear one of the guys call the other by the name 'Val' while we were in their office?" I asked Aimee.

"Yes, the cute one was named Val I think."

"There was a cute one?" Sally shook her head.

"Not by my book. They were both a couple of slick Willies thinking their *mierda* don't stink." Marisol put her thumb and index finger on her nose just in case anyone didn't know what "mierda" was in English.

"What are you thinking, Halsey?"

"I'm thinking, Peggy, that we have surrounded ourselves with two-faced liars. Liza Gilhooly, the commercial realtor I just picked up as a client, first said that she thought that one of the owners of the strip mall was named 'Valentin,' then this morning she recanted, saying that was the name of her CPA instead."

"Interesting. You don't have her real estate license number do you?"

I handed Peggy Liza's card.

"You can keep this. I've put all her info into my phone. Should we call Isabella and see how things ended up with Augie and Rico?"

"Yes!" everyone agreed.

I held the phone to the center of the car so that we could all listen.

"Hi, Isabella. I'm here with Sally, Peggy, Aimee, and Marisol. We're driving back from a meeting and wanted to find out how Rico made out with the police."

"Hi, everyone!" she said. "Did this meeting have anything to do with wine?" Isabella giggled.

She's in a giddy mood. I hope this means good news.

"Sadly no." Sally switched lanes probably out of frustration from no wine and being stuck behind a slowpoke driver.

"Aw, sorry, Sally. Rico is right here. Let me put him on."

"Good afternoon, ladies." It was nice to hear Rico's voice, although it sounded a little shaky.

"I take it you're a free man," Peggy said.

Rico sighed.

"For now, yes. Although my fingerprints match those on the dough hook."

"We expected that, right?" I asked.

"I suppose so, but I swore to Augie that I'd never been near that alley and I'd never seen the safe in my life."

"And Augie believed you, honey, correct?" Aimee actually reached out and tried to give the phone a pat. I pushed her hand away before she could accidentally disconnect the call.

"I wouldn't go that far, Aimee, but that was all the evidence he had so Augie let me go."

"You believe Rico, don't you, Marisol?" I looked at her for any indication of a subsequent conversation with her "dear" nephew, Augie.

She sat up tall and looked at me. "If it gets my wings back, yes."

"We'll get your wings," I said. "Sally, you were pleased with the work that lawyer did for Jimmy last year, weren't you?"

"Absolutely . . . she had him out of jail and the cops eating crow in no time."

"Great. Can you call her and see if she could look into Rico's case?"

"Heck yes."

"Ah, ladies. We do not have money to pay for a lawyer. Right now, we have no income flowing in and who knows how long it will take to get an insurance check . . . if ever, now that the cops pegged me as a suspect in the fire."

"Don't worry about that, Rico. We'll take care of it and you can pay us back when you can."

"Thank you, but I, we, can't take your money. We always pay our own way."

I could hear Isabella talking in the background.

"We're about to go into a tunnel and we might lose you," I pretended, and disconnected the call to spare the Brunos further embarrassment.

"Now who's a liar?" Marisol said.

It was a good thing that Sally still had the backseat child safety locks on from a recent visit by her nephew and his family.

I spent the next few days engrossed in work, not just for Liza, who frankly I'd lost my taste for, but also for my steady-paying clients. We could only barter so much, and this wedding wasn't going to pay for itself. Since this was my second time around, I could easily have forgone the gown and the other pricey traditions, but Jack would have none of that. I understood, but I just kept putting off looking for a dress.

Finally after lunch today, I decided to crack open

that book. We'd decided on the first week in June and reserved that date with Penelope for the winery. Since we were now into October, I figured that I'd better at least nail one thing down.

I wasn't going to fool anyone with the virginal look, so I started by looking at dresses with plunging necklines. I ruled out anything with too much frill or that exposed side boob. *That ship has sailed.*

When a general Google search yielded nothing but gasps and angst, I decided to look on J.Crew bridal. Shows you what I know; they stopped selling wedding gowns in 2017. The only other name that came to mind was Vera Wang, and I was pretty sure that I couldn't afford her designs.

I lucked out when I found an online outlet store that had prices within this stratosphere. I opted for a low-back gown with a spaghetti strap camisole with organza flowers sewn onto tulle and lace. Thank you, Vera.

I was reveling over my sense of accomplishment and commitment when there was a knock on my office door.

"It's open!"

The last person that I expected to see walk in was Augie. He wasn't a bad-looking guy, if a little slightly built for a detective. With the exception of a bit of a paunch that hung over his uncharacteristic themed belts that he mostly kept hidden under his standard-issue gray suit jacket. Today I could just make out that the brown, leather belt had embroidered LA DODGERS logos all over it.

"Whatever it is, I didn't do it."

"I didn't come to accuse you of anything, Halsey,

although I must admit you have a guilty look on your face."

"I shouldn't . . . I'm about to become an honest woman." I slid my chair back to let him see the computer screen and my wedding dress.

"You're getting married?"

"See, Augie, you're not such a bad detective."

He sat down at my conference table. Augie clearly had something on his mind.

"Can I get you a water? Coffee or tea?"

I was proud of my polite self.

"I'm fine thanks. But I have some news that I know you're not going to like."

"Is it about Rico and Isabella? You can't possibly think that you can build a case around a dough hook."

"It's not that."

"Then what? Spit it out, Augie."

"I had a meeting with Inspector Mason and his team this morning. They have determined that the fire's point of origin was in the attic that is open all the way through the mall. Some of the proprietors used it for extra storage. The fire was started above the drugstore."

"Okay, that should completely exonerate the Brunos. I can't imagine them crawling over six stores' worth of stuff just to point the blame elsewhere. And they'd have to crawl all the way back before the fire got to them. They are innocent."

"For now, maybe."

"And?"

"Mason's team found thick glass shards where the fire started and were able to piece enough of them together to determine that a so-called Molotov cocktail was used as the incendiary device."

"What do you want, Augie, a parade?"

"There was a label on this bottle—it was a wine bottle. They found enough to be able to decipher the name. It was a claret and it was from the Abigail Rose Winery."

"What did I just tell you, Augie? Penelope and Malcolm had flown in from their honeymoon and Andrew went to the airport to pick them up! All of this can be checked. Not one of those three could have started the fire, let alone have motive to. This time you've really gone too far."

"So how did that bottle get there?"

I suddenly remembered Penelope telling us that while they were away, Malcolm's cousin Andrew had worked out a deal with Rico's Pizza to serve wine in their parlor. I needed to subtly find out if they had any bottles in the restaurant at the time of the fire before I let this news put Rico back in the hot seat, no pun intended.

"I don't know, Augie," I finally said, "that's why you're the detective and I'm not."

Chapter Thirteen

"We can go after your Dionne Warwick special if that's what's bothering you."

"That was last week, and Sunday. Don't you get *TV Guide*?"

"I just need to test out a theory. We know we can't get in there during the day, so I need your help and your night vision goggles."

"And Bardot, you need Bardot."

I was standing on Marisol's front stoop talking to her through her black, wrought iron safety screen door. It always reminded me of being in the confessional, which was convenient because usually about halfway through a conversation with her I wanted to kill her.

"So what's your theory."

"You going to make me stand out here and tell it to you? What if someone hears us? I know Peggy wouldn't approve."

That got her. Marisol fancied herself right up there in the spying echelons with the former CIA operative.

"Hurry yourself, I don't want to let the flies in," she said, cracking the door open about six inches.

I squeezed through and stepped into her living room.

I'd been in Marisol's house before. There were always at least three TVs playing at once, and one played surveillance video from whichever house she was currently spying on. She claims that a young relative set this up for her, but I suspect that somehow she taught herself or had someone teach her. She could be very persuasive, and if I ever go to Vegas, I'm taking her with me to raise walking-around money.

I'd brought an iPad with me, and once she sat on her sofa, I sidled in next to her and fired it up.

No pun intended.

"I've been doing some online research about arson and arsonists and came across the name John Orr. He was a fire investigator here in California, working on arson cases around the late seventies and early eighties all over the state."

"What is this, history class?"

"Stick with me, Marisol, I'm about to get to the good part."

She hopped off the sofa and went into the kitchen. I heard rustling and rattling for a couple of minutes and then she returned with a bowl of movie theater popcorn and two Yoo-hoo bottles. For some crazy reason she was in love with the chocolate "drink." I tried not to look at the list of ingredients after popping the cap.

"Okay, I'm ready, you may proceed," Marisol commanded.

"This guy was really good at identifying the points of origin of fires, and he discovered that a series of blazes set in box home improvement stores were started by using a time-delay device. In these cases it was a cigarette with a rubber band around the end that held several matches in place. The slow-burning cigarette gave the arsonist time to get away before the device ignited the matches and whatever flammable products he had chosen as fuel to spread the fire."

"Pretty clever. Did this John guy catch the bastard?"

"That's the kicker. Investigators that worked with him started to realize that John Orr was always within driving proximity to each fire. And we're talking all over the state. It was when he was at a convention of arson experts in Fresno that a fire broke out in nearby Bakersfield. There was a fingerprint left on some notebook paper that had been attached to the incendiary device and it later proved to match John Orr's prints. When all was said and done, he was convicted of being a serial arsonist and mass murderer. Four people had died during one of his blazes, including a two-year-old little boy."

"Jesus Christo," Marisol said, and crossed herself.

We both sat silent for a moment.

"I'm still convinced that those creeps who own the building did this, maybe to empty the building of tenants, fix it up a little, and charge five times as much rent. You saw them the other day. Would you trust them?"

"Not as far as I can throw them."

"You saw computers all around their office, didn't you, Marisol?"

She nodded.

"Then if I could find out about this John Orr and his methods, so could they. And if they used a similar time-delay device, they could have been out of there before anything went up in flames. Being landlords, they probably had a key to the drugstore and could have set the device and then locked up again and left."

"What about that wine bottle they found, the one they used as a Mount Olive cocktail?"

Another Marisol malapropism. I hadn't had a chance to tell anybody about Augie's news yet, so how did Marisol know? I made a mental note to sweep my office for bugs and cameras again.

"Once the cigarette burned down, and the matches lit, they would have ignited the rag sticking out of the bottle. And whoosh. You very quickly have a hot, fast-burning fire."

"Whoosh." Marisol tried out the word for size.

Marisol had a point. I need to figure out how the mall owners got access to an Abigail Rose wine bottle or this all falls flat.

"Do you still have the business card you took from the Provident office?" I asked her.

She reached into her gaucho-style denim pants that looked kind of like a billowing skirt and pulled it out.

"Great, this is a long shot, but if one of those guys had handled the card, then I'll let Bardot smell it and we can see if she matches the scent from something in the burned strip mall. And we will also look for traces of the time device. The investigators just might have missed something if it wasn't top of mind."

"Roger that. We'll go at midnight."

"Why so late?"

"Because *Despicable Me* is on cable tonight, duh."

Figures.

We decided to drive up there because Marisol had all this equipment and we didn't want to attract attention to ourselves. A blond woman, an old lady, and a dog walking around after midnight was not exactly a usual occurrence. Especially when the wizened one was toting a bunch of spy paraphernalia.

I parked the car far enough down a side street to be incognito just in case a nosy Augie happened to drive by. In addition to the night vision goggles, Marisol carried a metal detector—for what reason I don't know. There would certainly be shards of metal everywhere. I let Bardot out the back and had her take a good long sniff of the business card.

"You might want to have her smell this too," Marisol said, producing a gold pen. "That one guy had been holding it and put it down on the reception desk."

"You stole it?"

"I thought that it was complimentary, like a parting gift."

As much as I wanted, I couldn't get mad at her. This could be the break we need.

"Smell this real good, Bardot, then we're going to go in there and you're going to lead me to something with the same scent. You understand?" Jack had a command for this, but I was drawing a blank. The last thing I wanted to do was call him because he specifically hated it when I broke the law.

I put a harness on Bardot and attached a long leash. In this case I needed to let her take the lead. When we reached the shell remains of the mall, we stopped at the section where the drugstore had been. I hadn't thought about how we were going to get up to the attic section of the stores, and I hadn't brought a ladder. I took a quick look around and saw a possibility. There was a structure next to the mall but a separate building that had not burned. There was a shed at the side of it that you could climb onto from the building's backdoor steps. From there it was a short hop to the mall roof and the ventilation holes that the firefighters had made into the attic.

"Okay, Marisol, you limit your search to what you can find on the ground floor of the drugstore. Here's a handful of baggies, so collect anything that you think might be useful and bag it with your gloved hand. I'm talking glass shards, cigarettes, matches, hair samples, anything that looks out of place for this kind of store. Got it?"

"This isn't my first rodeo."

"Most importantly, be safe. If anything feels wrong, you get out of there right away."

"Anything? Like you and Bardie falling on my head? Like *that* anything?"

"We're going to be super careful up there too. I only plan to step inside a short way and only onto metal beams."

"There'd better be some wings in my future."

I watched her step inside the gutted building, and then I hoisted Bardot onto the roof of the shed. Instead of being afraid, she seemed to think that this was the kind of adventure that she'd been waiting for her entire life. She wasn't being reckless. She seemed to recognize the importance of this mission. I must remember to ask Jack just exactly what he does with her when he takes her to the Santa Monica Mountains for night training without me.

I climbed up onto the shed as well and donned my night vision goggles. It was actually more like a pair of binoculars with a head strap, but the thermal imaging made objects appear as clear as in daylight. I wondered where Marisol got all this paraphernalia and what it cost. I figured that this was another one of her schemes she'd work with somebody on to get them for cheap. The jump to the roof of the mall was just a couple of feet, but this time I went first to make sure that there was something solid to stand on. When I felt safe, I commanded Bardot to hop up. Once on top, her nose started pulsating and working overtime. I let her smell the gold pen again. She wagged her tail and put her nose down to what was left of the attic floor. I tied one end of the long leash around my waist so that if she fell through, the harness would stay on and I could pull her back up. Assuming that I didn't fall with her. I spread my feet apart to get a steadier purchase of the beam below me. Meanwhile Bardot seemed to recognize that she needed to proceed with extreme caution.

"Find anything?" I heard a shout from below.

"Quiet, Marisol, or someone will hear you and call the cops."

"Just asking," she said in a softer voice.

Bardot started to gently tug on the line. We were getting close to the area where the firefighters had made a vertical ventilation hole. It was a clear drop from there all the way down to the floor.

"Slowly, Bardot," I whispered.

Pieces of debris fell off the edge as we moved closer to the opening.

"Ouch! You did that on purpose."

"Marisol, shhhhhhh."

Bardot stopped and started scraping away bits of roofing material with her paw. She was working harder than a cat with a fresh litter box. I crouched down to get a better look. Suddenly, she began a barking sequence.

Crap, I bet she's going to do this ten times.

Sure enough that was the count that Jack had taught her to do when she found her target. I bent over with my goggles and saw a piece of something that looked orange. I could hear a siren in the distance, so I quickly scooped it up into a baggie.

"Marisol, we have to go. NOW!"

We reverse-engineered our ascent, but this time I went first down to the shed and then helped Bardot with a half lift from me and a half hop from her. The marine layer had battled with the warmer evening air and won, making all the surfaces damp and slippery with dew.

Marisol was waiting for me on the back steps of the undamaged building when we got down. In her hands she held at least a half dozen filled baggies.

"Good work. Now quietly and slowly let's walk to the car."

The sound of the siren got much closer, and we looked at each other and broke out into a run.

I was not spending a night in jail with Marisol.

Chapter Fourteen

The next morning, I woke up late and as I padded into the kitchen to make tea, I scanned all the baggies that I had strewn across my living room coffee table. I was pretty sure that it had been Augie in that police car last night, but even if it wasn't he would have been told about possible intruders at the mall. Which meant that Marisol couldn't ask him to do any testing on our evidence without giving ourselves away.

I heard Jack's truck pull up outside and quickly scooped up the bags and hid them under the sofa. Bardot, also sleepy, thought that a game was commencing and got down on her belly to try to retrieve them.

"No, Bardot. Leave it. This is not a game. I am just cleaning up for a change."

"Hi, babe, you just get up?" Jack looked at his watch. "Isn't Penelope supposed to be here in like twenty minutes?"

"Yes, I'm just making some tea and then I'll dress quickly. I couldn't get much sleep last night, Jack."

"Aww, I'm sorry, darlin'. It's because I wasn't there to keep you warm."

He enveloped me in his arms.

What? I didn't lie, I hadn't had much sleep. That's the truth!

I put the kettle on and returned to the bedroom to throw on some clothes.

"Hey, I talked to Mark this morning, and he says that the DEA's got a lead on some pharmaceutical Oxy that's just hit the area. They were going out to investigate today. Somewhere by the beach in Venice," Jack shouted from the living room.

I also heard the chomping noise stop and figured that Bardot had finished her morning kibble. The sound of a soft burp confirmed it. Right about now I bet that she was ambling out the back to resume sleeping in the sun. Who could blame her? I only wished that I could do the same.

"Hello, luvs. Is that the kettle I just heard go off?"

"Your timing is perfect, Penelope," I said, coming through the hallway. We exchanged kisses on both cheeks. "Make yourself comfortable while I make the tea. I actually have some orange scones to go with."

"Excellent. Hello, handsome Jack. I bet that you've already had a full day of dog training. I know that you start even before the roosters crack an eyelid."

"That's true, Penelope. The best time to work with dogs is before they've had their breakfast and haven't eaten in about twelve hours. They'll do pretty much anything you command for a treat."

"You're marrying such a wise man, Halsey."

"He can't be that smart if he's marrying me." I brought in a tray with the tea and scones.

"I'm the luckiest man in the world."

Jack was sitting on the sofa under which I'd stashed last night's evidence. Which was a relief because it meant that it would stay firmly in place under his weight. Bardot came in after hearing Penelope's voice and gave her a smooch. She then went down on her back on the sisal rug and made serpentine undulations to thoroughly back scratch.

That's my family.

"All right," Penelope said, unpacking a stack of photos from her bag. Now that the date is set, we can start working on some of the details for your wedding. Having recently gone through this myself, it's all fresh in my mind, including the vendors we used."

Penelope laid out a series of pictures of table settings with floral centerpieces.

"These run the spectrum of very formal to more casual and natural."

"I'm casual and natural," I heard Sally say, popping her head in the doorway. "I saw Penelope's car out front and had to make sure that I wasn't missing a party."

"You're not and we could use your help, Sally. We're doing some wedding planning." I motioned for her to join us.

"Oh Lordy. Joe and I got hitched during the Carter administration and we were poor as church mice. It was held in his uncle's backyard, and in honor of Carter we had bowls of peanuts in the shell at each table for the reception."

"Sounds like my kind of party." Jack grinned.

We spent the next hour discussing and debating the merits of different florist styles, save-the-date cards, the guest list, the menu, and the entertainment. We really didn't settle on much as Aimee, also attracted by the cars outside my house, dropped in, adding another opinion and more fuel for debate. At one point I just looked at Jack and smiled. He mouthed the word *elope* and raised his eyebrows and shrugged his shoulders.

It was a tempting thought.

"I found this fellow waiting around outside and figured that he belonged to one of you," Peggy announced, leading Andrew into my house.

"Oh, Andrew, sorry we're running a tad late," Penelope apologized. "We rode in together so that he could chat with the Brunos about our joint venture."

"Come on in, you two. Is that still on, with the pizza place being out of commission?" I asked Andrew.

"Certainly our side of the bargain is. Isabella has worked out an arrangement with Aimee to use her kitchen space on off-hours to prepare and freeze individual artisan pizzas for us to bake and sell at the winery."

"That's what I was coming to tell you, Halsey," Aimee explained. "Isabella called me this morning to ask if they could rent some space in my store. Of course I refused the money, but she insisted."

"What a perfect solution," Sally beamed.

"And they want to buy a real pizza oven for our kitchen." Penelope clapped her hands.

"I thought that Malcolm was building an outdoor stone oven?" Peggy commented.

"He is, but Isabella doesn't want to rely on that to be the only resource."

Rico and Isabella must have gotten some insurance money . . .

My living room was now filled with people so, of course, Marisol waltzed right in.

"Is that all you're serving?" she asked me. "You're getting cheap in your old age."

"Cheap? I don't remember inviting—"

Bardot let out a growl, got down on her belly, and tried to shimmy under the sofa.

"What's up, girl, did your ball roll under there?" Jack asked, standing up. Sally and Andrew who were seated there as well followed Jack's lead.

"No!" I shouted, causing everyone to stop and stare at me. Except Marisol, because she had her head in my refrigerator and was scrounging for food.

"Sorry, I didn't mean to yell, but I'm working on Bardot's manners. She doesn't get to be the center of attention when I have guests."

"Ah, good point," Jack said, sitting down again.

Bardot kept trying to flatten her body to the width of a deli sandwich and was pawing at the space under the couch.

"Psst," Jack said, putting a stop to her machinations.

Marisol returned to the living room with a plate holding a sandwich and a pickle.

"You know, this is probably the first time that we've all gathered in one room without any open wine bottles," Aimee remarked, and the girls looked at each other.

"Too early for me. I haven't even had breakfast," I said.

Jack stood. "I've got to hit the road, babe. I'm working with a pair of whippets this afternoon in Westlake Village. Thanks, Penelope. I hope we were of some help at least."

"You were, Jack. Really."

"What we need is a Wine Club devoted to wedding planning," Sally declared.

"Brilliant idea," Peggy chimed in.

Great, the waters were muddied enough when everyone was sober.

"Your dog is staring at me, Halsey. Why is she doing that?" Andrew asked.

Jack had left and so had Bardot's manners.

"Maybe she thinks that you're an Afghan hound with that long curly hair, Andrew." Penelope laughed.

"Very funny. We should be getting back to Malibu. I know that Malcolm was hoping that I'd help him in the fields this afternoon."

Andrew got up, leaving only Sally to weigh down the sofa. Since it sat on the wood floor and not the rug, Bardot could push it back if she put enough muscle into it.

"Yes, we must be off. Thanks for the tea, Halsey. And ladies, don't forget the harvest is on Halloween, so get ready for a sleepover." Penelope gave me a hug.

"Sounds like fun," Andrew remarked, staring at me.

"Is it really one o'clock? I've got to get to the yogurt shop!"

"I'll walk out with you, Aimee," Sally said.

When Sally got up off the sofa, Bardot went to work on moving it. Peggy and I watched, and I must admit I was impressed with her determination.

"Why don't I just pick one end up; it's clear that she's not going to give up until she retrieves her ball," Peggy said, lifting one arm of the sofa into the air.

Bardot quickly moved in and started batting baggies away until she found the one with the orange piece of plastic that she'd tracked in the mall attic.

She then began her sequence of ten barks again.

"Don't you have any cookies?" Marisol asked, handing me her empty plate.

* * *

"I'm relieved to hear what these really are . . . for a moment I thought that I'd found your stash of crack cocaine bags."

I'd gathered up all the evidence and spread it out on the coffee table for us to review. Peggy picked up one that looked to contain some pieces of colored glass.

"The claret wine bottle is green. I saw it up close the other day when Jack and I drove up to the winery to talk about the wedding venue. I'm not sure where the other colors of glass would have come from."

"You ever go into that drugstore?" Peggy asked. I shook my head and looked over at Marisol as she did the same. I noticed that she was now enjoying my Jeni's Middle West Whiskey & Pecans ice cream.

"I'll have you know that that is a twelve-dollar pint of ice cream that you are inhaling, Marisol."

"It's good, but you're going to need to get some more though." She spooned the last bit of creamy, salty, butterscotch vanilla into her mouth.

"Ahem, back to the glass," Peggy said to focus us. "The store had a collection of old apothecary jars in different colors displayed on a shelf that hung on the side wall. I strongly suspect that is where these shards came from."

I was starting to think that this had all been a horrible waste of time. And I was getting a massive headache from not eating.

Peggy picked up a couple more bags.

"Who collected these?"

"I did. Halsey told me that if I found hair, I should bag it up."

"It looks like you found several different ones, Marisol. The blond one is pretty long, and not dyed . . . look at the root."

Peggy handed me the bag. I saw Marisol staring at my roots and gave her a threatening stink eye.

"I'm out. I need a nap," she said.

"Don't let the door hit you on the way out, Marisol."

"I can't hear you."

"If I ever kill her, which could be any day, I hope that I can count on you to provide me with an alibi, Peggy."

"You got it." She picked up another bag, one that had a long, dark hair strand in it.

"I'm trying to picture the staff in there. I know that the pharmacist was a bald man with glasses, but he did have at least a couple of assistants. Both women, if I recall."

I took the bag from her and held it up to the light.

"The fire was on a Sunday, when the drugstore was closed. I think that they close around four on Saturdays. The key thing to know is whether their janitorial staff comes in after they close for the weekend or before they open on Monday."

"I can check on that. I've got a couple of prescriptions that came from there and I have the pharmacist's card. I'm pretty sure that it's his cell phone that is listed."

I remembered Peggy's comment about getting old, a worrying thought.

"And we have this," Peggy said, examining the piece of orange plastic that I had recovered in the attic.

Bardot instantly stood up and watched Peggy handle the evidence.

"Believe me, I have stared at that thing and examined it under a bright light from every angle. I got nothing. The only way this could be of help would be if it tested positive for fingerprints and those prints were in the system to identify the owner."

"I can probably have the test done if I may borrow this for a while?"

"Sure."

"Oh, and my associate got back to me with what he found on this Liza Gilhooly. You ready for this?"

"I am, Peggy, but Marisol has just consumed every ounce of food I had and if I don't eat in the next ten minutes, I'm going to bite into a vein in my arm and suck out all my blood."

"Sounds pretty drastic. We'd better go then!"

Even though this was an "any port in a storm" dining emergency, the thought of melted cheese and corn tortillas had popped into my head and now it was that or bust. Really only ten minutes away, Paco's Tacos was the destination of choice.

For forty-five years this fine establishment has been serving the Mar Vista area with freshly made Mexican fare. The story goes that Paco Haro went from a modest taco stand to an eighteen-table restaurant that is so popular that you'll often find groups of people sipping margaritas in the lounge waiting for their tables to open up. Despite the taco place being open every day of the year. The menu offers everything from burritos to enchiladas to seafood and yes, delicious tacos. Staff freshly chopping pico de gallo and crafting tortillas from scratch are in full view to the diners. The Supermex Burrito filled with beef, avocado, beans, and topped with special green sauce and melted cheese is the fan favorite and exactly what the doctor ordered for me.

"I'll just have one chicken taco," Peggy said to the waiter.

"You usually consume a plate of food as big as your head, Peggy. You feeling okay?"

"I'm fine, just not much of an appetite."

I examined her demeanor. She was a tad pale and when I caught her eyes she looked downward. She was holding back from me.

"Peggy, is there something about your health that you're not telling me? When was the last time you saw your doctor?"

"Last week . . . I waited forty-five minutes only to be put into an examining room to wait another thirty. Drives me batty."

"What did he say after you finally saw him?"

"That I looked tired and he was going to have a nurse run some tests. He was out in less time than it takes me to tinkle."

"That's frustrating. When are they supposed to call you with the results?"

"Tuesday or Wednesday."

"That's not too bad. You'll let me know as soon as you hear?"

"Yes."

"Promise?"

She nodded.

"Hey, maybe what we need is a couple of margaritas. It is Sunday after all."

Peggy shook her head.

"The doc wants me off the sauce until he can determine what is going on."

"What a drag. And I'm sure that a little glass of wine or something would relax you and stop your worrying."

"As long as this is only a temporary teetotaling sabbatical, I'm okay with it."

The waiter brought our food. Peggy's looked like a reasonable, light lunch for the health and weight conscious. Mine looked like a green speed bump used on a road that only allows semitrucks.

"Anything else?" our server asked.

"We're probably going to need more chips and salsa, and refill on our waters."

Peggy looked at all my food and smiled. I cut out a large piece of tortilla, meat, and cheese and placed it on my tongue. It was so good that I had to close my eyes.

"Should I let you savor your meal, or do you want to hear about Liza Gilhooly?"

"I can do both. But you need to eat too."

"I am."

Peggy had barely touched her taco. She pulled an iPad out of her bag.

"She's quite a piece of work, this one."

Peggy pulled up a file on her tablet.

"She's had two bankruptcies, was sued for illegally trying to evict a tenant from a commercial property—which was eventually settled out of court—and has had tickets for moving violations as long as your arm."

"I've seen her drive so I'm not surprised."

I thought about the eviction suit, and it brought to mind again how the burned-down building gave the owners a chance to tie things up long enough for the old tenants to jump ship and go somewhere else.

"Liza claimed to me that she only knew the owners of the strip mall by reputation and perhaps a casual meeting or two. I've already caught her in a couple of lies, so maybe she knows them better than she's letting on."

"Sounds like it." Peggy agreed. "Any chance that one of those hair samples could be hers?"

"Hah! Her hair is processed more than Velveeta cheese. If it was her hair, I would have recognized it right away."

"What about that surfer kid? The one that had the auto parts shop?"

"Now he's a possibility, he's a natural blond, and his hair is even lighter from being in the sun and saltwater all the time."

I looked down at my empty plate and didn't know whether I should be proud or ashamed.

"And of course Roberto had dark hair."

"Yes, he always had it slicked back, so I'm guessing that a strand could have been long. Speaking of which, I guess that Rico and Isabella got their insurance money already."

"I don't think so." Peggy studied my face. "I ran into her at the bank on Saturday and she was still complaining about more red tape and paperwork that the assessors were demanding."

"But Penelope said that they were going to buy a pizza oven for the winery. How can they do that if they're crying poor? Those things can't be cheap."

Peggy nodded. "Got to be at least ten grand even if they buy one used."

"Well, this is just great."

We'd begged off dessert and were presented with the check. I made a mental note to take a run to Whole Foods later for Jeni's ice cream.

"What's great?" Peggy asked, taking a look at the bill.

I quickly grabbed it from her. "This is my treat—you barely ate. What's great, but actually stinks, is that we have a number of very credible suspects who could have caused that fire."

"Liza Gilhooly," Peggy started the list.

"The strip mall owners, if we can nail them down and get their names. Then there's the theory that Brandon and Roberto may have worked together to claim insurance money and Roberto couldn't get out in time."

"And sadly," Peggy added, "the Brunos aren't looking so innocent either. Unless they have a valid source of money to pay for that oven."

"Don't forget the police finding the safe that once held opioid drugs. Though circumstantial, that dough hook from Rico's was found with it in the alley. With Rico's fingerprints on it."

Peggy reached in her pocket and pulled out the baggie with the piece of orange plastic.

"I have a feeling that this is the key to unlocking the entire case," she said, and I nodded.

Chapter Fifteen

The next morning was spent combing the Internet for matches to the object that Bardot had found in the attic. I'd decided to work off of theories, so I started first with the elements used in making pizza.

I looked at pizza dough cutters and while some had colorful plastic handles, I didn't come across one that resembled the orange evidence piece. I moved on to serving supplies with even less luck. Lastly, I delved into the components of commercial mixers, electric cheese graters, dough presses, and ovens but had no "eureka" moment. When that fell flat, I moved on to lighters and fire starters. I found some items that looked close but nothing that looked like an exact match.

Finally, and in hopes of tying Brandon to the fire, I went to my local Pep Boys auto supply of the "Manny, Moe, and Jack" fame. Started in 1921 by four navy buddies for just eight hundred dollars.

The place was as daunting to me as Ulta Beauty would be to Jack. After bombing out in four departments and exhausting as many salesclerks, someone suggested that this might be some sort of tool used in packaging. That meant taking a trip to Home Depot, another mega store and another possible wild goose chase. As I got into the car my cell phone pinged and I saw that it was Sally.

"Hi! You are a bright shining light in an otherwise rotten morning."

"That bad, huh, girlfriend?"

"If you don't know where you're going any road will take you there, Sally. And I feel like I've covered most of them."

"Oh dear. I have some news, and I'm just leaving Venice beach. You want to meet up back on Rose?"

"You know what? I'm near the beach too and I've just decided that I've followed my last empty road for today. Want to meet for lunch somewhere?"

"If the creek don't rise, sure would! How about Cha Cha Chicken on Ocean?"

"Perfect, see you there in twenty?"

"Not if I see you first."

Sally and her expressions.

I felt only a modicum of guilt for blowing off another hour roaming around Home Depot "hangry" (hungry making me angry). Plus, I had something important to ask Sally that for some reason I kept putting off.

Cha Cha Chicken is basically a colorful take-out stand, with its corrugated metal sides painted in Caribbean yellows, blues, reds, greens, and blacks. I could sense the Bob Marley vibes even before I stepped onto the patio. One of the things that I love about this place is that it's tucked just far enough away from the

Santa Monica Pier to be off the radar of throngs of tourists. I spotted Sally perched atop a bar stool, her long, caramel legs draped around one stool leg.

"I already put in my order, so go get yours, girl-friend, and I recommend the mango-guava water."

With the sun shining down on her, I half expected a Rasta man with a steel drum to walk by and say, "Welcome to Jamaica, mon." In deference to yesterday's Bacchanalian repast I opted for a lighter fare of roasted chicken in spiced Jamaican jerk sauce and a cup of black bean soup.

"Everything smells delicious, but I can't believe that I can even think about food after the gorging *fiesta* I had with Peggy yesterday."

"She pigged out?"

"Hardly. I'm the one with the curly tail."

I wondered if Sally knew more about Peggy's health than she was letting on. A number was called and Sally went up to get her food. She stood talking to the person behind the trailer counter, and a moment later she was handed another plate that must have been mine.

We tucked in and I let the fruity, spicy flavors linger on my tongue.

"I wonder what kind of wine would go best with a meal like this," Sally mused.

"Hmm, if we're not having Red Stripe beer I'm guessing a crisp white, but it needs to stand up to the intense flavors of the food." As I said this I pictured myself lounging at a café table on a terrace overlooking a cornflower blue lagoon.

"So with a rich, grape flavor and zesty texture." Sally nodded.

"Would you listen to us, do we not sound like total wine snobs?" I laughed.

"These plantains are like manna from heaven. Try one."

I speared one from Sally's plate, thereby relieving her of the burden of falling short of joining the clean plate league.

"You said you had news?"

"Yes, I think that you'll find this interesting, Halsey. I went to the fire station this morning to pick up some sand bags for the upcoming storm and then stopped off at the beach to fill them. The church always floods, and I wanted to make sure that they're prepared. While I was in the process of scooping sand, I saw the same sweet paramedics that I'd just talked to pull up. I guess at this time of year, and due to budget cuts, there are no lifeguards on duty early in the morning. I watched them unload some gear and then heard one of them say, 'Guy who called it in says the victim's name is Brandon Dawson. That's twice this month we've had to save the kid. He should give up trying to learn to surf.' Can you believe that?"

"It must have been a different Brandon. Isabella told me that all ours does day in and day out is surf." I took a sip of mango-guava water and swilled it in my mouth.

"I thought you might say that, so I followed the paramedics to the shore to offer my nursing services. The kid had certainly been beaten up first by a wave and then by the rocks underneath, but they soon had him sitting up and breathing in oxygen. While everyone was busy, I took out my phone and snapped a photo. I've never seen the kid before, but is this the fellow you met, Halsey?"

Sally showed me her phone screen and there, looking like a half-drowned mutt, sat the Brandon I knew. Right down to the tattoos on his hands.

"That's him alright, but I'm scratching my head about the fact that the kid can't surf. Penelope even said that Malcolm's cousin Andrew would go out with him whenever he was on the Westside. Does that mean that Andrew isn't a surfer either? And if so, why lie about it?" And what were they doing together each time if they were not out in the ocean?"

"I'm afraid that this news only serves to muddy the waters more. This case is as difficult as trying to find a lost ball in high weeds."

I had to laugh at another of Sally's crazy expressions. Bless her heart, as she would say.

"Sally, I wanted to ask you something."

"So you said on the phone. Anything!"

"As you know, Jack and I have set the date for our wedding. He's decided to ask his friend Mark from the DEA to be his best man, and I would be thrilled if you'd be my maid of honor."

"Shut the front door, honey. I wouldn't miss it for the world. Come give me a hug."

Sally's is not quite as cocoon warm as Peggy's fleeced bosom, but she throws in the rocking thing to make up for it. We spent a good couple of minutes shutting out the world.

"Sally, is there something wrong with Peggy? Healthwise?"

"You sensed something, didn't you?"

I nodded and my stomach sank.

"She found a lump on her breast, but thankfully she went in right away and they did a biopsy. We're waiting for the results. She confided in me but didn't want anyone else to know in case it was nothing."

"God, poor dear. Do you think that it will be nothing?"

"It's hard to say; this was very early detection, which in itself is a blessing. But the statistics are against her, all of us actually. I don't mean to alarm you, especially since you are about to get married, but one out of eight women have a risk of being diagnosed with breast cancer in their lifetime. Now if it's caught early it is very treatable, and most women go on to live long, healthy lives."

"I suppose that's good news."

"Before you start getting your bloomers in a twist worrying about Peggy, this is commonly a slow-moving cancer in women in their late eighties, and she'd go from natural causes before the cancer would become an issue. Still the major key, as I told all my patients when I was a nurse, is early detection."

"That's a depressing thought. Do they sell wine here?"

"I believe that it's BYOB, honey. Let's not get upset about something before it happens . . . we're still waiting on the biopsy results."

"I understand, but it's just, well, sickness is not my strong suit, especially in people I really, really love."

"Whatever happens, we'll handle it, Halsey. All of us Wine Club girls are invincible, you know that."

Sally rubbed my back for assurance. I sure hoped that she was right.

* * *

When I pulled back into my driveway, I saw that there was Marisol plunked on my front steps. Oddly I thought that maybe her lunacy would help lighten my mood.

"You've been gone long . . . what'd you do, drink too much at lunch and have to sleep it off in your car before driving home?"

It might have been working. Just hearing her cackling voice was making me smile. The sun was directly in her face causing it to blur to an oval halo, so I couldn't really make out her features. I noticed that she had a large baggie filled with something resting on her lap.

"Don't tell me you went back to the mall during the day and scraped up more evidence. I told you how dangerous that would be. You couldn't be that stupid."

The moment that last set of words escaped my mouth I regretted it.

"Nope, but I scraped something else instead."

When I reached her my body blocked the sun, and I could see that Marisol had a growing, swelling black eye that looked like it wanted to take over her head. I looked down and saw that the bag she'd been holding was filled with ice and was resting on a bloodied knee.

"Oh geez, what happened? Who did this to you? Want me to call Augie?"

"Nobody did nothing, so don't call Augie. I was walking and I fell."

"Can you stand? I want to get you inside and have a better look at your injuries."

She made an attempt to put weight on her legs and fell right back down. She had tears in her eyes.

"Nope, okay we're going to Emergency."

When Marisol didn't argue, I knew that this was bad.

She must weigh all of one hundred pounds soaking wet, so I was able to lift her up and help her hobble toward the driveway. I opened the back door and eased her onto the seat of my car. Bardot barked from the backyard and I responded, "I'll be back in a bit honey."

I started the engine and before backing out called Aimee. I put my phone in the dock so that I could talk on speaker and drive safely.

"Hi, honey, are we having an impromptu Wine Club?" Aimee asked, picking up my call. "I know it's only Monday but—"

"Does Tom have a shift today?" I asked, cutting her off.

"Yes, Halsey, he left about twenty minutes ago. Why?"

"I'm bringing Marisol in. She says she fell walking, but her injuries seem too serious for that. Can you call him and let him know that we're coming?"

"Oh dear lord, of course."

Tom, Aimee's boyfriend, is an ER doctor at St. John's hospital in Santa Monica. Everyone there is great, but it always helps to have someone you know on duty. A sudden wave of emergencies could mean waiting for hours and hours to be treated.

"Do you have any of Marisol's daughters' phone numbers you can call and let them know?"

"I'll take care of it so you just worry about getting Marisol in Tom's hands. Oh dear, this is terrible."

I ended the call and sped up Twentieth Street to the hospital. Unfortunately, I knew the route well. Sally was taken there after she was shot a few years back, I spent some time in its ward recovering from a concussion, and last year Peggy's beau Charlie was taken to St. John's following a small plane accident.

That served as a reminder of Peggy's pending diagnosis, and I started to worry all over again. It seemed as though my world was imploding.

Chapter Sixteen

Sure enough, there'd been an accident with a city bus and an SUV, and the waiting room was packed. I scanned the area for any sign of Tom. When I didn't immediately see him, I grabbed one of the last remaining vacant wheelchairs and pushed it back to my car. I'd left it with the valet in the loading area of the Emergency Room.

"Can you help me get her out and onto the chair? She can't put weight on her leg," I told him.

"Sure."

The valet set the brake on the wheelchair and peered into my backseat. His automatic movements told me that he'd done this once or twice before.

"I don't need no hospital," Marisol growled, causing the attendant to jump back from the fearsome noise and the creature that made it.

"Don't worry, she won't hurt you," I assured him. "Your tetanus shots are up to date, right?"

"Ha, ha, ha, you funny, Halsey."

That last scary squeal from Marisol sealed the deal, and I lost the valet to another car and patient. The valet and I made eye contact, and he hung his head down hoping for absolution.

"I don't know how long I'm going to be, so can you park it on the top level?"

He nodded. This was the kind of help that he was comfortable with. Clearly, he'd never held a job as lion tamer with the circus.

When Marisol took one look at the commotion in the room, she tried to get up and walk out.

"You sit and stay," I commanded her in a strong but pleasant voice just like Jack had taught me. Sure enough Marisol calmed down.

"Goood girl!"

"Shut up, Halsey."

"Hi, Marisol, tell me what hurts the most," said a voice approaching behind me.

Seeing Tom made me feel instantly better. Apart from knowing that he'd become a great doctor, Marisol was a cougar in her own crazy way and she always behaved better around nice-looking younger men.

"Hi, Tom, thanks for finding us. Marisol said that she was walking and tripped, but I suspect that she hasn't told me the entire story."

"On my death bed you call me a liar, Halsey?"

People stopped what they were doing and stared at the crazy old lady in the gardening clogs.

"We're tight on rooms and equipment at the moment, but let me take you back, get your vitals, and do some preliminaries. Aimee talked to your daughter, Martha, and she's on her way to be with you."

"I feel better already, thank you, Doctor."

I watched him wheel Marisol through the double doors that separated the waiting area from the emergency treatment rooms. I had to admit to myself that it stung a bit that once she saw Tom and heard that her daughter was on her way, I just vanished into thin air as far as Marisol was concerned.

But that was our relationship; we shared a tough love. I stood where they'd left me for a moment, watching as spouses, significant others, and relatives poured into the room to be with their loved ones. I figured that I'd wait until Marisol's daughter arrived and then take off. When it came right down to it I wasn't family, and I couldn't make any medical decisions on Marisol's behalf. I spotted one empty seat in the far back corner of the waiting area.

I called and let Sally and Peggy know what was going on and promised to keep them informed as soon as I heard anything from Tom.

About five feet from me and suspended from the ceiling was one of about a half dozen TVs tuned to a local Los Angeles news station. I gave it my focus hoping that it would numb my mind a bit.

They were showing the exterior of a wonderful and majestic church in south Los Angeles, the kind of architecture I'm used to seeing in Europe but rarely, if ever, in California. The closed caption feed crawled along the bottom of the screen so that I could read what I was looking at.

St. Vincent de Paul Catholic Church is a designated historical-cultural monument on West Adams Boulevard not far from USC. The church, designed by architect Albert C. Martin and funded by local oilman Edward J. Doheny, was built in the early 1920s. At that time the West Adams district was one of the wealthiest areas of the city.

The video moved now to closer shots of the façade.

Done in the Spanish Baroque style of elaborate sculptural
and architectural ornament, it is remarkable in its extreme,
striking, decorative florid detail.

The camera then entered the church to reveal one
of the most spectacular golden interiors and altars
that I'd ever seen. I was at once mesmerized and over-
whelmed with a sense of great emptiness.

It was clear that no matter how close I was to
Marisol . . . I was not family. In times of trouble I had
to take a backseat to her immediate family. I had to
accept those rules, and the hurt reminded me of just
how much I really do love her.

That got me thinking about Peggy, another friend
on Rose Avenue whom I consider family. She is so
clever and full of energy, and the thought never
crossed my mind that with her advanced age came
advanced illnesses. If Sally is correct, and I have no
reason to doubt her expertise, even a positive diagnosis for cancer would be slow to manifest itself. But the
lid to the pot had been opened and I was now much
more aware of her mortality.

And my bestie, Sally, while a true-blue friend, has a
husband to take care of, in addition to her valuable
work with the youth at her church. My family—my
wonderful parents, aunts, uncles, and cousins—were
all four glasses of wine, a meal, a snack, and one in-
flight movie away.

Thank God for Jack, although technically we
weren't family yet because we weren't married. And
the wedding seemed so far away.

I turned my attention back to the video, which was showcasing some of the intricate details of the church's apse.

The mental inventory of my life had made me exhausted, which sent me into slumber land.

My reverie was interrupted by a visit from Tom. "Hi again. I wanted to give you an update on Marisol. She's banged up pretty badly, and there is some fluid on her knee. But it is the blow to the head that we're most concerned about. The neurologist has ordered a cranial CT scan and we may follow up with an MRI. We're in the process of admitting her. Her daughter Martha is with her. Marisol did admit that her fall was 'maybe more like being hit by a car,' she wanted me to let you know, but she refuses to talk to the police."

"I knew it. I bet that she was back snooping around the burned-down strip mall. Tom, do you think that she's going to be okay?"

"She's responding well to stimuli, but she has some cognitive irregularities, shall we say. The tests will tell us if there are any signs of dementia."

"How well do you know her, Tom?"

"Hardly at all, just from chatting for a few minutes at parties and barbecues."

"Then I'll let you in on a secret. Marisol was born with 'cognitive irregularities,' and they may just put her in the genius category."

I thanked Tom and he promised to call with any news. There was nothing more that I could do, so I headed out the back of St. John's hospital.

The parking area had calmed down somewhat. I'd witnessed the last of the bus accident victims go in for treatment, so there was no longer a frantic arrival of concerned people. The same valet that was on duty before brought my car up and held the door for me.

"Thanks, how much is it?" I rescued my wallet from my purse. I'd been there for over two hours, so I searched for twenties.

"No charge; you were here for an emergency," he said.

I had seen other people paying when I arrived and again just now.

"You're a good man," I said to him, and he bowed his head.

Before I pulled out of the circular drive, I grabbed my phone and speed-dialed Jack.

"Honey? How soon can you meet me? I have something important that I want to ask you."

Chapter Seventeen

A couple of days later, we convened for Wine Club at Peggy's house. I tried not to look at my phone all morning, dreading seeing a text from her canceling the event, which would definitely mean that she'd gotten her test results and it wasn't good news.

I hadn't been told about any theme to this gathering, and I didn't want to bring something that called out "special occasion," in case it wasn't, so I made some understated pumpkin hummus and brought along pita chips and apple slices. And crumbled bacon.

When I arrived, a little early, Sally was the sole guest so far. Peggy was in her kitchen, and the place smelled of maple, pie, and cinnamon. A good sign I thought. It was confirmed when I noticed that Sally was laying out champagne glasses on the coffee table. I gave her a questioning look, and she gave me a thumbs up and then pantomimed locking her lips. I gave her an understanding nod.

"Halsey! Welcome to my fall Wine Club feast." Peggy gave me a warm smile. "Oh, and I heard from my doctor and the tests revealed nothing serious. I just have to make some lifestyle changes . . . starting tomorrow!"

I grabbed her in a tight embrace. The two-day throbbing headache that I'd been dealing with released a little tension off my brain. "But come tomorrow, missy, I'll be all over your butt. And after Wine Club today I'm going through your freezer, pantry, and anywhere else you could be hiding processed sugar and trans-fat."

"Oh joy. Sally, should I fly in the kids and all my grandbabies for the event?"

"Hi! I brought little hazelnut galettes filled with chocolate and pear frozen yogurt. I'll put them in the freezer until we're ready, Peggy." Aimee marched in grinning, in her element after creating new recipes.

"I thought that we'd start with a little Piper Heidsieck Cuvée Brut to waken up the old taste buds and then move on to a couple special reds that I coaxed out of my wine merchant for a great price."

"Sounds dreamy, Peggy," Sally said, passing around the filled flutes.

Try saying "filled flutes" three times fast after you've consumed a few.

"We've got a lot of business to cover today besides imbibing, and I am going to run this meeting in the hopes of keeping us on track and productive. Otherwise it's my house and I'll kick out the lot of you and keep this wonderful spread all to myself."

"The day of reckoning is tomorrow, Peggy."

"Thanks for reminding me, Sally. First and foremost, we know that Marisol is home from the hospital and recuperating, but how's she doing, Halsey, and what was the final diagnosis?"

I quickly finished the strawberry that I'd been luxuriously dipping into my champagne.

"As you would expect, knowing Marisol like you all do, she's been a model patient and a joy to take care of and be around."

Sally raised one hand, held her thumb under her other four fingers, and dragged it out from her nose as far as her arm would reach. Her whistle sound effect let us know that she was pantomiming a cartoon Pinocchio telling a lie.

"Okay, not really," I continued. "The good news is that she'll be fine, the Marisol definition of fine. The neurologist didn't detect any real signs of dementia, but he also couldn't understand the way her mind works. I suggested that he go to Stonehenge for the answer."

"Thank goodness . . . Tom told me how worried he was when he first examined her."

"He was great, Aimee, and as soon as he took charge she started to behave herself. The bigger concern, perhaps, is that through lots of coercion and bribes I got her to admit that she was walking around the back of the burned strip mall when she fell. She claims that she was watching a car drive through the alley, trying to see its occupants, when she tripped over a concrete parking space stop."

"Ouch, no wonder she was so banged up. Did she at least get a peek at the driver?"

"Unfortunately not, Peggy. And she really didn't have much of a description of the car, but she insisted that 'if she saw it again she'd recognize it.'"

"I'll stop in to check on her this evening and see if she remembers anything more," Sally said.

"Does anyone have an update on the Provident building owners or on your commercial real estate client, Halsey?" Aimee sat up proud, taking ownership for our surprise visit to the corporate office in Downey as well she should.

"This will blow the lids off your collective noggins." Peggy stood up. "I talked to my friend who is helping with identifying the owners of the cars that were parked in that office building, and he said so far most could be tracked to people that legitimately work there. But there was a section of the video where the sun played tricks on displaying the license plate numbers. He happened to have someone in the field nearby and asked her to check out the garage, find those models and makes of cars, and take down the tags."

"Wow, Peggy, talk about the long arm of the law. I hope you're going to tell us that they now have the names of these shady real estate owners."

"I wish, Halsey, but this might be just as interesting. The field agent decided to take a stroll past the Provident Commerce Group offices on the off chance that she would run into one of the owners. Sure enough the double doors were open, but when she stepped inside all she saw were maintenance and construction workers. Those guys had moved out practically overnight and taken any evidence that they'd been there with them."

"That makes me madder than cut snakes!" Sally spat, and then emptied her champagne glass.

"Sounds like it's time to uncork the Coppola Diamond claret."

That did the trick, and we were now getting very excited for our night in Malibu. We discussed the other open issues in the case with not much in answers.

Q: How can Rico and Isabella afford to buy another pizza oven prior to receiving the insurance payment?
A: Maybe they could borrow against the payment? Or they got an advance?
Q: What is Liza Gilhooly's connection to all this and why was she lying to us?
A: Peggy suspects that she is a street fighter by nature and stands to get some money out of the fire whether it is from something she did or something she knows.
Q: Where is Brandon and what role did he play in all this? Why lie about being a surfer and what is his connection to Andrew?
A: Could it be as simple as trying to meet girls?

As the sun set at an increasingly earlier time each day as we were coming to the end of October, we Wine Club girls had done a good job of polishing off the refreshments and delightful appetizers. Now more than a few eyelids were starting to droop.

"Madam chairman," I directed at Peggy, "have we sufficiently covered the items on your agenda for today's meeting?"

"I am satisfied, save for one more topic."

Several women groaned, but Peggy continued unfazed.

"In less than a week, we'll all be at Penelope and Malcolm's first fall harvest and, if I counted correctly, we'll be a party of nine, since Penelope opened up the sleepover to husbands and significant others. Charlie's flying up so that's two; Aimee, you'd said that Tom made sure that he wasn't on call, so four; Sally and Joe, and Halsey, Jack, and Bardot."

"Maybe my cousin Jimmy as well but he has to let me know," Sally informed the group.

"So that's a lot of people descending on them all at once."

"Right Peggy, we need to make things as easy as possible plus celebrate their amazing achievement of growing their first crop."

"Oh my, what do we get the couple that's just become vintners?" Aimee literally scratched her head.

"I'll call Penelope in the morning and find out the sleeping arrangements and if it would be easiest for us to bring our own bed linens and towels."

"Perfect, Sally." Peggy started a list.

"And I can take care of dessert. I'll do some fall pies and maybe candied apples and cheese."

"Please don't talk about food right now, Aimee." This time I really am committed to never eating again.

"And I'll take care of getting us a supply of the things that you never realize you need until you don't have them: flashlights, gloves, cases of water, those throwaway ponchos for the forecasted rain."

"Geez, Peggy, we're going to a sleepover in Malibu not a tour in Mogadishu." She gave me a look that let me know that I'm bordering on insubordination. "And I'll do some research and find the perfect wine-warming gift for them."

Peggy was satisfied and we came together for a final Wine Club cheer. I was the last to leave, and when I reached the door Peggy handed me the baggie with the orange piece of evidence.

"Wiped clean, Halsey. My guys got nothing from it."

When my eyes opened from sleep it was still dark outside. That didn't stop my brain from kicking into gear and start reviewing the mall fire again.

Aimee had told me that Rico and Isabella were going to be using the kitchen on Thursday night to complete their final prep before the big harvest and suggested that I pop by if I wanted to get information about their finances and plans.

I got up early to get in a walk and then a swim with Bardot before it got too hot. The forecast called for powerful Santa Ana winds this afternoon, and that always meant trouble. It is said that the name comes from a Native American word for wind, which Spanish missionaries, detecting an evil presence, translated as "Santanás" or what we call today the "Devil Winds."

When I'd first heard this I thought that it was some kind of Californian myth, but then I experienced three days of Santa Anas and knew of what they spoke. Upon waking you are deceived by seeing the cloudless blue sky that this is to be another day in paradise. Then you notice that during the night someone practiced using sandpaper on your lips and had you chew on dry Grape Nuts cereal. You get up ready for a fight and decide to take a telemarketing call just for practice. Then you curse everyone who has ever said with a smile, "But it's a dry heat."

There's an eerie stillness in the atmosphere and a positive ion-driven ebullition in your hair. Then the fires start, little scattered pockets that encounter each other in travel and join forces ultimately turning the sky into a blanket of orange and gray. It looks like a giant Hermes shopping bag has landed above the city. This is followed by migraines and fatigue that are only exacerbated by alcohol. This is why God invented books, and air-conditioning, and beds to enjoy them in.

I made the call about halfway through our walk that our time in public was over for today. My plan was for a quick dip and a long nap before heading out to Aimee's yogurt shop. Bardot had no arguments with the itinerary.

As we rounded the corner, Bardot picked up her pace and wagged her tail with excitement. I guessed that she was looking forward to leaving the outside swirl of positive ions as well. This day was going to turn out just fine.

Then I saw Augie standing in my driveway.

Bardot was beside herself with happiness and I was gearing up for a fierce contest.

When we got close he gave me a big smile, and I could see that he was holding a bag weighted down with something heavy.

"Whatever evidence you think you've found on me, Augie, is just another one of your bumbling mistakes. I've done nothing wrong and I'm not in the mood for you. Can't you see that the Santa Anas are blowing?"

"This isn't evidence and I'm not accusing you of anything, Halsey." He looked crestfallen. "I just wanted to thank you for taking such good care of auntie Marisol, driving her to Emergency, and making sure she got help right away. She told me all about it."

Maybe that old witch does appreciate me.

"It's a big bag of candy; I'll just leave it on your

front steps. There is some chocolate in there, so I'd advise you to bring it out of the sun right away."

This had to be some reverse Devil Wind phenomena. Instead of people getting meaner, they were getting nicer. I looked at Augie and wanted to hug him.

I didn't.

"You'd better come inside as well, Augie, and I'll fix you something cold to drink. Are you on duty today?"

"No ma'am."

"Excellent, then that something cold will have alcohol in it!"

"Wow, sour cherry rolls, Bit-O-Honey, saltwater taffy, Mary Janes—I love those—licorice bulls-eyes, peanut butter cups, gummy handcuffs? Never seen those before . . . you sure know your stuff, Augie. This is a great gift and I really appreciate it."

I really did. We were sitting in my living room because it was too unpleasant to be outside. Augie had a beer and I couldn't let him drink alone, so I sipped on a Sancerre.

"Where do you get this yummy, nostalgic stuff?"

"There's a place on the Venice Boardwalk where they have walls lined with filled bins and scoops, and you choose what you like, they weigh it, and you pay accordingly. You can find crazy stuff in there too like a five-pound gummy bear or a one-yard-long chocolate bar."

"And you went there just to get this for me? I'm touched, Augie. May I get you another beer?"

"I'm fine for now, thanks. I didn't just go there for candy. I've been working the parking areas and side streets for a group that have been ripping off people disguised as help when someone's car won't start. Or has been damaged or they have a flat tire."

"Ripping off how, if they're getting the person back on the road?"

"It appears that the same guys that offer to help are probably causing the trouble in the first place. They show up looking like they've just come from surfing, boards in tow and wet from the sea. One of the guys has some parts in his car and they make the repairs. The victim goes to the ATM and in spite of their refusals pays them handsomely. They mostly target the elderly and tourists."

Thoughts were stirring in my brain.

"Wouldn't this be something that falls under the jurisdiction of the Beach Patrol?"

"Normally yes, but they've been able to trace some of the parts to a small distributor that sells only to the Westside, Mar Vista, the Marina, and Culver City. All my areas."

I weighed the up and down sides of telling Augie about Brandon's beach rescue and lack of surfing acumen. But he's supposed to have been surfing with Andrew and I don't want to put a spotlight on Penelope and Malcolm until I know more. This could be nothing.

"I hope you catch them, Augie. Preying on the elderly, that stinks, but tourists, not so much."

"Halsey!"

"Sorry I said that; it must be the Santa Anas."

This time I did hug him. We were family after all.

Chapter Eighteen

Despite the fact that I own a full-size SUV, Jack still looked a bit cramped driving my car. Although, good sport that he was, he didn't seem to mind.

We were driving east and north toward areas where the first settlers lived in Los Angeles and the surrounding areas. We left the cool ocean breezes behind and I shut my passenger-side window and adjusted the AC.

I loved old Los Angeles and its rich history, and felt like a dry sponge wanting to sop up stories and points of interest that I could spend years exploring. Unfortunately, murders and websites kept getting in the way. *And a wedding.* Still I spent last night up late getting to know the place where we were headed.

"Did you know that Richard Ramirez came from Eagle Rock?"

"Who's that?" I seemed to have awoken Jack from a Zen state.

"The 'Night Stalker.' Back in the eighties he went on a killing spree, and they attributed fourteen murders to him spread all over the Valley."

We took the exit and then merged onto the 134 Freeway that cuts a C-section across the Valley.

"Remind me again why we're going to Eagle Rock, Halsey?"

"To pick up this antique vineyard wine corker that I found on the Internet. It will be our gift as a group to Malcolm and Penelope to celebrate their first harvest."

"Are we going to someone's house? Couldn't they have shipped it?"

"Jack, it is cast iron, so it would cost a fortune to send it. And no, we're going to a wine-making supply outlet. And also, the 'Night Stalker' was caught."

"That's a relief."

We had reached Burbank and passed first Disney and then Warner Bros. Studios. Where the magic happens.

"For that case, yes." I decided to string Jack along.

"There are more?"

"The 'Hillside Stranglers.' They go back to the seventies, when they raped and murdered ten people including two teenage girls."

"How do you know all this stuff?"

"I like to read up on places that I'm visiting for the first time so that I know what to look for."

"And that was all you found about Eagle Rock? Murders and rapists?"

"Of course not. Did you know that there is actually a rock there with indentations that cast the shadow of an eagle in flight?"

"That makes sense. I need to take you on all my long drives . . . you are a wealth of entertainment, Halsey. What else can you regale me with?"

The traffic thinned out a bit as we drove past Griffith Park and the Observatory and the LA Zoo. Kids were in school and supposedly everyone else was at work on this Friday, otherwise we might have sat on the blacktop for hours.

I filled Jack in on my conversation with Augie and the interesting case he's working with the Venice Beach Patrol.

"Why has this captured your attention? Because of the auto parts angle? Just because Brandon owned one doesn't mean that he's behind these scams. He'd be too busy surfing."

Jack looked at me and I continued to stare straight ahead.

"Halsey?"

"What?"

"You're not telling me something."

"No, I'm not."

"Look me in the eye and tell me you're not holding something back."

"You need to keep your eyes on the road."

"A marriage works best when there are no secrets between the man and the woman." Jack grinned at me.

"Who told you that?"

Silence.

"Okay, Jack."

I told him about Sally's encounter with the paramedics and Brandon.

"Wow, that sure throws a different light on things. And you didn't tell this to your new best bud Augie?"

"I didn't want to throw shade on Andrew until we have all the facts. From what I know Brandon could be working this scam with any number of his beach bum friends. Plus, why would Andrew want to ever waste his time with this type of short con? I'm sure he makes good money at the winery . . . or will be soon."

"True, but you never know what lengths people will go to."

"Jack, you're supposed to be Mr. Positive."

"I am. I said 'people,' not dogs."

The last leg of our journey took us through Glendale, and its famous Galleria shopping mega mall. Think back to the movie, *Valley Girl,* and Valspeak phrases such as: "As if," "Fer shur," "Whatever!" and "Gag me with a spoon." Words that have seeped into *Merriam-Webster's* dictionary like black mold into the walls after a pipe leak.

Finally, we pulled off the main drag and into the town of Eagle Rock and took a windy road partly up a hill before Siri told us to turn off. The place was a big, metal warehouse with doublewide opened doors that led into the cavern. From the number of cars in the parking lot, I guessed that this place was a popular destination for oenophiles.

The temperature dropped about ten degrees when we entered the space. If it hadn't been for the signs suspended from the rafters, we would have had no idea what we were looking at. There were things called de-stemmers and crushers; they kind of looked like photocopiers with a vegetable scale attached to the top. We perused the presses, some of which looked a bit like a barrel with a broom handle in the middle and others looked like the kind of coffee urn that they would wheel into the ballroom at the Hilton for the CPA conference.

By pure luck we wandered into the corkers and cappers section where I was to ask for a fellow named André. I looked around for someone in a green apron, which I'd noticed was what the helpers wore. Jack provided another set of eyes.

"We're in luck," Jack said, using his redwood height to search in a much wider area.

"You found help?"

"Even better, I found Andrew."

Before I could stop him, Jack waved and called out his name. I'd hoped to get in some useful spying before we made ourselves known.

"Jack! What on earth brings you here? You got Halsey in tow?"

Jack picked me up and held me at shoulder height.

"You do that again and you'll be singing falsetto, Jack."

He quickly put me down.

We met Andrew halfway. Today his long curly mane was held back in a low ponytail and his jeans and T-shirt made him look more like the boy next door rather than the lothario at the bar. He shook Jack's hand and gave me a respectful peck on the cheek.

"So what brings you out to this hidden emporium of all things viticulture?"

"We're picking up a gift to present to Malcolm and Penelope to celebrate the harvest. The entire Wine Club chipped in. But it's a surprise so don't say a word."

"That's very kind . . . my lips are sealed."

"How'd you become so knowledgeable about wine-making, Andrew?"

"It's a bit of a story, Jack. What do you say we head over to the tasting room where we'll be more comfortable and more quenched?"

Jack looked at me and I nodded. Already this was more words than I've ever heard Andrew mutter.

We perched on stools at a bar-height wooden table while Andrew arranged for a tasting. He returned followed by a green-aproned guy carrying a tray of wine flights.

"I've had these before and they are all delicious," Andrew said to the server. "Please allow me to introduce them to my guests."

The guy nodded and left.

"This first one is from Los Olivos; it is a Syrah produced from the very fine Beckmen Vineyards. A very elegant wine."

"Lovely, Andrew."

Jack nodded and kept sipping.

"You asked about my background in wine. To be honest I never really liked it in my youth. I was more of a beer and bong guy growing up."

This was a bit of a surprise to me, because in spite of his hair I never took him for a "Bill" or "Ted" type.

"Where were you raised, Andrew?" Jack had finally come up for air.

"Northern California, so getting into winemaking was pretty much inevitable. I was in foster care and wanted more than anything to get down here where the water's warm and so are the ladies. Every summer I worked long hours at a local winery and did as much overtime as they'd let me so I could save enough to head out on my own. After high school graduation I took my diploma and my used Honda Element and pointed the car south."

"Wow, that was awfully brave of you. Did you know that Malcolm was down here at the time?" I asked.

"Not at all. Shall we try the Bordeaux-style blend from the central coast?"

"You didn't know where Malcolm was or you didn't know he existed?" Jack snuck in a probing question.

"A little of both, I guess. We lived in the same neighborhood, more of a hippie enclave if you want to know the truth. After Malcolm's parents died in a car crash, he came to live with us. We were already a blended family and one more wasn't going to make a difference. That is until the money ran out, then we kids were parceled out to homes in the system. I lost track of Malcolm and everybody else."

"Oh, Andrew, I'm sorry. That sounds like a rough start to life." I put my hand on his arm. He responded by putting his other hand over mine.

Jack cleared his throat.

"You still haven't told us how you and Malcolm reunited after all these years."

"Ah, yeah. It was all his doing. I guess that Malcolm had been knee-deep in a project tracing his lineage. The same project that ultimately led him to his great-grandmother, Abigail Rose. He picked up a trail on me and ran it all the way to Venice Beach, where I'd been living."

"What must that have been like, seeing someone you hadn't seen in what, twenty-five years?"

"It was surreal. And then to learn that we were actually blood relatives, second cousins, that was crazy, Halsey."

"So you settled in Venice Beach, and what were you doing for a living? Something with wine?" Jack was like a dog with a bone . . . even though he'd released my hand, he was losing his patience with Andrew.

"In Venice? Nah, I worked at a body shop on Lincoln Boulevard. And finally, let's taste the port."

* * *

For the first twenty minutes of the drive back we rode in silence. Jack had one hand on the wheel and the other scratching at his beard, the telltale sign that he was upset. I wasn't exactly sure what the cause was; in the time I'd known him he'd never been the jealous type. And this was nothing but innocent empathy for someone who'd been dealt some lousy cards. If Jack was going to freak out any time a male laid a finger on me, then we have a serious problem.

"Jack—"

"Halsey—"

"You go first," he said.

"Something is bothering you. Ever since we left the warehouse you haven't said a word. And you've worn a bald patch in your beard."

He quickly flipped down the sun visor to inspect his face.

"Are you going to tell me what it is, Jack? I thought you said no secrets."

"As you probably guessed, it's Andrew. I don't trust the guy and I think that he was trying to pull one over on us with that story today. I hate when people think that they can outsmart me."

"Why would he lie? He must know that we could verify everything with Malcolm."

"That's what really galls me—he is so arrogant."

"Hmm, I actually thought that he seemed genuine and human today."

"I've never known you to be gullible, Halsey. Is it because he's good-looking?"

"What? You need to look at your face in the mirror

again. You're the one that's good-looking, and you two couldn't be more polar opposites."

I saw Jack's shoulders relax and his face soften.

"I'm sorry, babe. It's just that there's something about Andrew that isn't right."

"Do you know what is right?" I asked as we turned onto the 10 Freeway heading west.

"What?"

"A shrimp cocktail, a martini, and a steak at Chez Jays."

"I love you." Jack beamed.

Chapter Nineteen

You would wonder with all the shenanigans that I've been up to how on earth I was able to finish up Liza Gilhooly's website. Well, between us, I'd written some of the main components of the database years ago and just update it when needed according to operating system and browser upgrades.

Liza had agreed to come to my office this time. She told me she felt guilty for the neglect and wanted to make it up. She was even bringing lunch. For the first time we were experiencing a real fall day, heavy misting marine layer, gray skies, and for us Angelenos—of which I now count myself—it was cold outside.

It was mid-sixties but that presents a chill when you're wearing flip-flops.

This was the fun part of the process. I knew that she'd be dazzled by the functionality and all the bells and whistles. I'd taken all the specs and requirements she'd given me at the start, simplified them, and gave the site smooth, elegant functionality.

There was one important aspect missing, however. The site had no personality whatsoever. Since she had wanted to hold off on adding a logo to the top of each page, I used a very generic illustration of an office building. The color scheme was pleasant enough in soft greens and yellows, but from looking at the site you'd never expect to encounter platinum Liza and her pink Cadillac. That worried me, but thankfully those cosmetic changes were fairly easy to make.

I gave Bardot a quick refresher course in etiquette and manners when guests come to call, and she seemed willing to comply.

"Knock, knock, helloooo?"

Liza came bursting in, and I noticed right away that she was back to her cheery self both in mien and sartorially. She carried a picnic basket and was adorned in a leopard print, long-sleeved cat suit over which she had draped a khaki calf-length vest. And I must say that she carried it off pretty well.

"Welcome to my humble office and Bardot's pool house."

"Oh, Halsey, it's beautiful, I wouldn't change a thing! Hello, beautiful."

I opened my arms for a hug and saw that her salutation had actually been directed at Bardot. My girl responded in kind by shimmering on the wood floor and displaying her hoohaw in all its glory.

"Don't you love this weather? It's getting me ready for Paris," Liza said, finally turning to me for an embrace.

"For one or two days, yes, but then I want it to back to normal. This puts a damper in Bardot's pool-diving activities and a bored dog is trouble . . . Paris?" I asked.

"Pool-diving?" she asked.

"Silly me, Bardot has a waterproof undercoat, so she's impervious to cold water as long as it isn't frozen over," I explained.

We both laughed. Upon listening to our conversation, Bardot started hopping up and down and whimpering at the French doors that lead out to the pool.

"I guess I better let her out before Bardot gets so excited that she springs a leak or something."

We followed her out and she went around to the farside of the pool and went into a down state waiting for further instruction. Without Jack being nearby, pool time was the only time that Bardot gave me one hundred percent attention and obedience. The reward of diving was so great to her.

I picked up two of her sinkable toys and held them up to her. One was a ring and one was bone shaped. I tossed one after the other into the deep end and saw that they landed on the bottom about a foot apart.

"I'm so excited. What is she going to do, Halsey?" Liza squealed.

"You're about to find out."

Bardot was about ready to jump out of her skin.

"Look at me," I said to her. "I want you to get the ring, Bardot. Go get the ring."

With that she dove softly into the water, barely causing a ripple, and we watched until the last yellow tip of her tail disappeared.

"My goodness, should we save her? I'm not wearing waterproof mascara."

Just then Bardot's head came up for air, and she blew water out of her nose just like she'd seen dolphins do.

"She's got the ring! She understood you, Halsey. I've never seen anything like that, Halsey. Bardot's a rock star."

Liza's voice had risen to a pitch rivaling choirboys'.

Bardot presented her quarry at Liza's feet, and I rewarded her with a couple of biscuits. She then found the sole patch where the sun had broken through and made herself comfortable for her snack and then snooze.

"Shall we go in? I'm really excited to show you your website, Liza."

"Sure," she said with about as much enthusiasm as she'd have for a dental technician.

I was starting to get concerned that perhaps Liza had buyer's remorse and didn't see the value in having a website for her business, which could lead to not paying me for my services. I thought back to the bankruptcies Peggy's agent had uncovered and wondered if I should brace myself for an uncomfortable outcome to this meeting.

We sat at my conference table, and she uncovered a tray of tea sandwiches that she'd had in her basket along with a bowl of delicious-looking fruit salad.

"Before I forget, here's your check. If there are any overages just let me know and I'll write you another one."

That took me by surprise.

"Don't you want to see what I've done first?"

"I'm sure that it's fabulous, you just hold on to that." She patted my hand.

I took her through the site and she was duly impressed. The squeal came back when I showed her how she could tap into and customize the property listings feeds.

"So are you good with the look and feel? The color scheme? I'll still need your logo and a photo and bio for you."

"That won't be necessary, Halsey."

I looked at her, confused.

"You see, I've made some big life changes since we last spoke. I've sold my business, to a competitor actually. He's aware of the website and what he's seen he just loves. I'm sure that you'll have plenty of business from him in the future."

"Wow, I didn't see this coming. What are you going to do, Liza?"

"I'm moving to Paris!"

"You have friends there? Business?"

"A bit of both. A beau from my past, a Frenchman, has just moved back there from California. We'd rekindled our relationship in the past month, and he's invited me to join him. He's also in commercial real estate, so once I get my license over there I can work in his firm. How perfect is that?"

Suspicious is actually the word that comes to mind. Which gave me an idea.

"That's so exciting! I'm sure that you and Valentin will be very, very happy."

"We will."

Then Liza caught herself and shut her mouth. I was about to get to the truth when the door burst open.

"Halsey, we've got to do something. They've taken Rico again and this time in cuffs!"

Aimee's chest heaved as she got the words out. Isabella followed her in, crying.

"What are you talking about? Who took Rico? Augie?"

I got out my phone, ready to call and rip into him.

"No, not Augie. Other cops, who were with that fire inspector, Mason. You've got to do something. Isabella is falling apart, and we can't let Penelope down. We've got to finish prepping for the harvest."

"Sounds like you've got your hands full, Halsey. I'll just slip out. *Bonne chance!*"

Before I could even say anything, Liza was out the door. I figured that was the last time we'd see each other, and I hoped that the check was good.

"Come in, both of you, and sit down. I need to know all that happened before we do anything else. Aimee, can you call Peggy and Sally and see if they're available? I have a feeling . . . this is going to require all the Wine Club brains."

Aimee busied herself setting out wineglasses even though we were technically still in the lunch hours. Isabella wrestled with a bottle opener but was too distraught to get the job done.

"I hope there's wine at this function," Peggy announced, entering my office. "I need something to take away this chill."

"It's sixty-five degrees out, honey, why didn't you wear your fleece?" Sally asked, following Peggy inside.

"There's wine, although it's a tad early for imbibing and we need clear heads to work on this riddle."

I relieved Isabella of her opening duty and motioned for her to take a seat at the conference table.

"It's chart time," I said, grabbing a large pad of paper. We'd had success with this exercise in the past;

it was a way to cover all the suspects, all the evidence, and all the holes. From there we would narrow down the list and make plans to go after what we still needed to know. Everyone contributed and when we'd covered everything, I stepped back to take in the chart:

Valentin and the other property investors: The only people that had actually seen them in the flesh were Marisol and Aimee. (I'd been hidden in the trash bin.) Isabella and Rico had never met them, because the only interaction they'd had was with the building manager. Isabella provided the manager's name, a Mr. Felix Juarez. The rent checks were all written to a trust company.

Action required: Track down Mr. Juarez. Peggy— see if she can get anything more on the trust company.

Conclusion: Since they have emptied their offices and since Liza Gilhooly let it slip that she was moving to Paris to be with Valentin—the name one of the owners called the other—it is a fair assumption that they have left the country.

Brandon Dawson: Stood to gain a fairly substantial insurance payout by the auto parts business being burned to the ground. Much needed if the store was on the brink of bankruptcy. He was supposed to be surfing on the Sunday of the fire, but Sally discovered through the paramedics that he has no talent for the sport. Concurrently, Augie is pursuing a scam case with the beach patrol that involves guys posing as surfers that provide assistance to the elderly and tourists with car troubles. Problems that the "surfers" created by removing essential parts from the vehicles in the first place. They just happen to have spare parts in their van and can fix anything on the spot for cash. Some of the parts have been traced to a distributor that services Mar Vista and the Westside.

Action required: Need to find something that ties Brandon to these crimes. Halsey and Sally volunteer to hit the beach early in the morning in the hopes of catching Brandon in the act. Also need to try and clear up why Halsey saw him go back in the burned building the day after the fire and then disappear out the back. Did he steal the safe so he could sell the opioids?

Conclusion: Many things point to Brandon as the arsonist. He had the means and the motive. But this car repair scam could be entirely separate from the fire and just a petty crime that he does for cash. Question whether he had the sophistication to research delayed incendiary devices by researching John Orr's history and crimes.

Cousin Andrew: Penelope thinks that he knows Brandon and said that Andrew loves to surf. Andrew had a rough childhood, grew up in foster care. Met Malcolm after his parents died in a car crash and Andrew's extended hippie family took him in. Later they separated and Malcolm was also sent into foster care. In his youth he worked in a winery. As soon as he graduated

from high school, he headed to Southern
California and got a job apprenticing with a
local auto mechanic. He says that Malcolm
found him when researching his ancestry and
living on Rose Avenue. Brought him into the
winery. And there is the matter of the fire being
set using an Abigail Rose wine bottle.

Action required: Confirm that Andrew actually
does surf. Try to get details on his relationship
with Brandon.

Conclusion: Andrew didn't have means, motive,
or opportunity to set the fire. He was at the airport picking up the honeymooners, Penelope
and Malcolm. After that, he was at the block
party the entire time. He has a great job at
what is sure to be a successful winery with lots
of opportunity for advancement and possibly a
partnership position.

This last one was tough to do with Isabella in the
room, but it had to be done.

Rico and Isabella: Lost their entire business in
the fire. They were delivering pizzas to the
block party just before the fire started. The
timing suggests they couldn't have been in two
places at the same time, and there were lots of
witnesses to attest that they were at the party.
Dough hook piece found with broken safe
from drugstore several blocks away. Confirmation that it came from the pizza parlor. And the
latest evidence, the Brunos just purchased a

ten-thousand-dollar pizza oven and had it shipped to the winery. Insurance hasn't paid out yet, and Rico won't say where the money came from.

I turned my attention away from the chart and sat down next to Isabella.

"Can you help at all, Isabella?" I plead with her. "You must have a sense about your finances. You've told me that you've earned barely anything since the fire, so did Rico cash in an investment to buy the oven?"

"Proof of that would sure clean things up in a hurry, honey." Peggy sat down to console Isabella.

"If he did, it was something that didn't involve me. We had a vacation fund that we set up with our bank at the beginning of each year, but we used most of it when we went to Italy in July. The only other savings is an IRA that we pay into. It requires both our signatures to make any changes, so I don't think that the money came from there."

"This Inspector Mason is not like Augie. We can't really push him around or force him to give us evidence," Sally groused.

"True, I'm the one that knows him the best and while he can be cordial, he takes his job very seriously. As he should, he deals in arson. And Isabella, Rico won't tell him where he got the ten grand?"

"Halsey, Rico is old school Italian and a very proud man. There are things you don't talk about, and showing weakness and needing help is a very low point for men like him. However he got that money he did it for me, for all of us, and it took everything out of him to do so. I worry that he doesn't have anything left to fight this with."

Isabella slumped inward, and her shoulders began to rise and fall with the tears.

Aimee got her some water and we all shrugged. I know we all felt so helpless.

Chapter Twenty

After a restless night worrying that Rico could end up going to prison and breaking Isabella's heart, I decided that we couldn't just sit anymore and do nothing. Augie was moving at a snail's pace and time was not on our side. I called Sally as soon as I got up, knowing that she'd be up and out doing her steps.

"Ready to do some recon with me?" I asked.

"Honey, I was born ready . . . Lord willin' and the creek don't rise."

Venice Beach is a different kind of place early in the morning, at least atmosphere-wise. As expected, we couldn't escape my driveway without letting Marisol tag along. It didn't matter the hour, she caught sight of Bardot hopping into the back of my SUV and slid into the backseat before I even knew it.

"We're only going to the vet, so why would you want to leave the warmth of your nest for a routine errand?"

"No, you're not." Marisol crossed her arms, sending a clear signal that she was not budging.

"Yes, we are, Marisol. Why would I lie to you about that?"

"Because you drink too much and you are a liar.

And also because here comes Sally and she's wearing binoculars. You're probably going to need to borrow some equipment from me, and if you ask nicely I'll consider it."

"Morning! I'm so excited . . . I'll get my steps in and enjoy some time at the beach." Sally hopped into the passenger seat. "Did you both apply sunscreen? Even with the marine layer you could get burned."

"Liar, liar, pants on fire."

I was busted.

"No, it's true, Marisol. Here, use this stick on your nose; it's greaseless."

"Thanks. And I was talking to Halsey. You I trust."

"How are you feeling, Marisol?" Sally used her concerned, nurse voice. "You were only discharged from the hospital, what? A few days ago?"

"I got good genes, and I don't know what the fuss was all about anyway. But I did pick up some good supplies while I was there." Marisol gave Sally her gold-toothed grin

"Supplies?" I asked. "Never mind."

For all I knew she could have marched out of there with an entire set of surgery tools.

It was fun driving the streets at this early hour when even the most ambitious workers hadn't left the house yet.

"So what's the plan when we get there? Want me to remove a part from your car, Halsey?" Marisol stuck her head up between the two front seats and looked from Sally to me and back again.

"Just how do you know about this car trouble scam, Marisol? The doctor told you to rest, and you wouldn't disobey his orders, would you?"

"You don't know what the doctor told me to do, because that's privileged information, Halsey."

"You were spying around my office when we were meeting yesterday, weren't you?"

"What meeting? Are you still hungover from last night?"

We reached the western most end of Rose Avenue, which actually dead-ended at the beach. We found a place to park at a lot that was currently without an attendant. Depending on how long we stayed we might get away for free. In high season a parking spot was second only to a seat on the stock exchange, and fees could easily be over thirty dollars.

Last night Jack had helped me figure out the best time to catch the most surfers and introduced me to surfline.com. When he'd first moved to Southern California, he'd caught the surf bug just like every other young man. He claimed that during the year he'd surfed almost every day, and he'd swallowed enough seawater to fill a bathtub. The site told you when the tides would be low and high, the surf height, wind direction and velocity, and the size of the swells or waves. There are even beach cams to show you the conditions in real time.

So a little after five thirty we disembarked from the car and headed down to the shore.

"The plan is to check out the people surfing first to see if Brandon or Andrew or anyone else we recognize is among them. If we spot anyone, we stay out of sight but follow them when they get out of the water. If we don't see anyone, we move to where the most cars are parked and keep a close eye, particularly on old ladies walking their dogs on the boardwalk."

"Got it! And I brought my binocs to make it easier to see the guys way out there on the water."

"Aren't you going to let Bardie run, Halsey?"

"It's Bardot, Marisol . . . and no, not here. If she's caught off-leash there's a hefty fine to pay."

"Then why'd you bring her? Seems kinda cruel. Like smelling fresh donuts but the shop is closed."

We found a spot under the lifeguard tower (which was unoccupied) and set up our surveillance in semi-obscurity. We watched young and old guys riding the waves and wiping out. A couple of girls braved the briny foam and easily threw shade on some of the men. The sun had just peeked up behind us, and Bardot was happy to snuggle up close to me and take in all the action.

"You see anybody you know, Halsey?"

"Not a soul, Sally. It could be the wrong day, the wrong time, or a host of other things. This was really a stab in the dark."

"So we go back to the cars and see if we can catch those creeps in the act?"

"I guess so, Marisol."

"Cute dog. You got somebody out there or are you just spectating?" came a voice from outside the tower. All we could see were a pair of hairy legs and the back of an upright surfboard.

"Who said that?" Marisol cackled.

A head appeared in the open space under the stilts where we had gathered.

"Hi, it was me. I'm Eddie."

"Pleased to meet you, Eddie. Was that you I saw crushing it out there?" Sally asked, and I wondered where she'd picked up the surfing lingo.

"Maybe, every wave's different. Sometimes I surprise myself in a good way or a bad one."

Eddie crouched down and joined us under the tower. He had unzipped the top of his farmer John wetsuit that ended at his thighs.

"So, who's out there that you're watching? Maybe I know him?"

Bardot stood, did a downward dog stretch, and ambled over to sit by Eddie. Moments later she was licking the salt off his arms.

I can't take her anywhere.

"You might know him . . . them. We came by to surprise them. Do you know Brandon Dawson?" I decided to go for it.

"That's your friend? He's the last person I'd expect that you nice ladies knew."

"What's he done, the dirty rat?"

I gave Marisol a look for that.

"It's more what he doesn't do. He can't surf worth sh . . . shells, he cuts us off, and he's dangerous out there. I saw one guy wipe out because of Brandon. He caught the rocks and needed a couple of stitches. We told him not to come here anymore, especially when the conditions are so good. Luckily, I haven't seen him in weeks, so maybe he got the message. Oh shells, what am I saying, he's your friend."

Eddie looked at us with an apologetic shake of his head.

"Don't worry, he's not a friend. In fact I'm the only one who's ever talked to him," I explained. "This is more about finding out what he's up to when he comes to the beach."

"Is he running scams?" Marisol blurted out.

"Not that I know of, but what kind of scams?"

Marisol was about to respond when I butted in.

"It's not important. Eddie, do you happen, by any chance, to remember if you saw Brandon surfing here on Sunday, the twenty-third, last month?"

"I remember the date because that was the start of a week of the best waves for the month. Five-, six-, and seven-footers. I don't think that Brandon was here, so maybe he's finally gotten the message."

"What about a fellow named Andrew?" Sally asked. "Tall, dark, curly long hair like Fabio?"

"Nope, never seen a guy like that on the water. Where's he from?"

"He works at a winery up in Malibu."

"Malibu? Then if he were a real surfer he wouldn't bother driving down here. Heck, he'd drop in the water at Surfrider for sure. Yeah, it's between the Malibu Pier and Lagoon. It has a super long break, and the guys that ride there are serious surfers. It's kind of a club that protects the waves." Eddie crawled out from under the tower and went into a classic surfer stance on the sand, with both feet planted one in front of the other, knees pointing forward, and arms wide and loose.

"It sounds like we're headed to Malibu, ladies," I announced. "Thanks, Eddie. You've been a great help and you're a rock star out there."

"*Vaya con dios!*" He grabbed his board and sprinted toward the water.

Bardot started whimpering and getting restless when she saw that we were driving on PCH. The smells of the Malibu Hills were beckoning her; she probably thought that we were meeting Jack and going on a wonderful adventure.

We were, minus Jack.

"This looks like a good place to pull over and park, Halsey."

I looked to where Sally was pointing. Now this is what beach movies are made of. The sun had come out, the water was as blue as Bradley Cooper's eyes, and the endless summer boys were seamlessly riding the curls. We did a U-turn and I slipped into a spot along the beach line. Even before I'd cut the ignition, Marisol was out the door and hopping down the sandy incline toward the shore. This got Bardot practically apoplectic.

I put on large sunglasses and a baseball cap in an effort to disguise my appearance, but of course the presence of Sally and Bardot were a sure giveaway.

"Let's just hang back here, Sally. With the sun up we should be able to find Andrew by his hair alone."

The waves were super big and powerful and ran quickly parallel to the shore until they died out just north of the Malibu pier. There were so many people out there I wondered how they seemed to manage just barely running over each other as they surfed. There was definitely a code of conduct for these guys, and I can imagine that the punishment was pretty harsh if it was broken. Almost everyone was wearing a black wetsuit, with or without sleeves.

"How the heck are we to spot Andrew in this crowd. Sitting on their boards out there, they all look like bottles of root beer bobbing in a trough of ice water."

I was impressed . . . that was a new one for Sally.

"From what I know of Andrew he doesn't do things

halfway. He has a healthy ego, and I doubt he'd put himself in this environment if he couldn't be the star. Let's watch for someone to take center stage, so to speak."

Just then Marisol appeared, plopped down next to me, and proceeded to suck on a Popsicle.

"Where'd you get that?"

"I have friends."

"Here you have friends, Marisol? Really? You conned somebody for that ice, didn't you?"

"I don't know what you mean," Marisol said, and offered Bardot a lick. They kept alternating until the they hit the center stick. Both Marisol and Bardot now sported cherry red mouths.

"There we go; that one's a hot dog." Sally raised her binoculars to get a better look.

I looked out and spotted a guy standing on his board and riding the very top of a big wave. Or, could this be a woman? The body was slim, long hair blown back behind the ears by the wind. It was really hard to tell. Whoever this was, he or she was a surfing master.

"That looks like Andrew to me," Marisol said, and Bardot turned her attention to the water.

"Me too," said Sally. "He's got those broad shoulders and sharp facial features."

I looked again and as the surfer got closer to the shore, it was hard to argue that this wasn't a man. He effortlessly maneuvered up and down the barrel to get the longest ride of anyone else out there. He was showboating.

Bardot emitted a growl.

"Poor Bardie, she really wants to get close and feel

the water. Please, Halsey?" Marisol gave me a wide grin and her gold-capped tooth caught the sun.

"Okay, you can walk down with her." I handed over the leash. "But don't you unclip her under any circumstances."

Sally clapped her hands and I saw that the star surfer had hit the end of his ride and slowly sank into the water.

"That's definitely Andrew," Sally said, focusing her binoculars.

I tried to make a positive ID as I watched the surfer hop onto his board and start to paddle back out. "Are you sure, Sally?"

All of a sudden, I saw a yellow dog splash through the surf, reach the guy, and grab a mouthful of the surfboard's leash.

"Never mind. That's definitely Andrew, and Bardot is towing him to safety."

I saw Marisol at the water's edge being careful not to get her garden clogs wet. Bardot's leash hung across her neck.

I pictured myself strangling her with it.

When Bardot had pulled Andrew and the board fully onto the sand, she stood back and started to ten-sequence bark.

"I guess we're busted, so we'd better go and take our lumps." Sally got up gracefully from the sand.

"Not necessarily. Follow my lead, Sally."

"Always."

"Fancy meeting you here." I waved to Andrew as we approached. "Bardot must really care about you, jumping in and pulling you to safety like that."

As I passed Marisol I yanked the leash from her

shoulders, and a bit of the leather strap snapped at her neck.

Oops. Way to go, Halsey, kick 'em while they're down, she just came out of the hospital!

She cringed a bit, but Bardot was safely tethered again.

"One word from you and I'll tie you to a board with this leash and set you adrift," I whispered, pretending to give her a hug. "I mean it."

"Yeah, that was quite a shock. I've never seen a dog out here, not sure they're allowed."

"Totally my fault. We'd just come from a training session with Jack up in the hills and I wanted to reward the girl with a refreshing dip before we headed home. You remember my friend, Sally, don't you, Andrew?"

He nodded. Some of the guys in the water were calling his name and whistling.

"Hi, Andrew. You really don't know how much of a workout you get climbing around in the forest. I've already done fifteen thousand steps today." I noticed that Sally wasn't wearing her pedometer.

"Well, we've got to get back. I've got a ton of work to do and Marisol has promised to wash my car."

She gave me a look and I raised my eyebrows at her. She backed down.

"Good to see you, Andrew. You really are a surfing super star." I grabbed Marisol's arm and spun her around to face PCH. Bardot seemed happy to leave after having successfully completed her exercise.

"Ta-ta, Andrew," Sally said. "You're the big kahuna. Cowabunga dude!"

Chapter Twenty-one

"I can't believe that I'm saying this, but I think that we need to meet with Augie."

"I can't believe that you're saying it either, Halsey." Sally looked to me for a reason.

We were headed home, with both Bardot and Marisol snoring in the back of my car.

"Care to elaborate?" Sally persisted.

"It's time for information sharing. I feel that there are too many parties involved, all following different leads, and it's time to rein them in."

"Give me an example."

"Okay, Sally, we know that Brandon can't surf and has been lying about his prowess on the waves. Augie doesn't know this yet, and he is investigating short cons involving auto repairs done at the beach with parts sold in Mar Vista. What can we glean from all of that and where should we go from here?"

"Right." Sally picked up the train of thought. "And Inspector Mason who is responsible for catching the arsonist must also deal with the stolen safe filled with opioids from the drugstore. The same safe that was found in the alley with a piece of dough-making equipment that had Rico's prints all over it."

"And finally, we've got the drugs themselves, which could fetch a ton of money on the street. To my knowledge the only ones tracking that are the DEA and Jack's friend, Mark. Finding out who is selling them could explain Rico's sudden cash flow . . . reprieve or exonerate him completely."

"Right. So what would be a reason to bring cops, fire inspectors, and the DEA together in one room, I wonder?" I could see Sally raise her eyes skyward in concentration.

"Donuts," came a squawk from the backseat.

"You just had a Popsicle. we're not stopping again, Marisol."

"No, you dope. Donuts will bring them all together and I have just the place."

I was starting to be able to read Marisol's insane mind. Scary.

Primo's donuts, on Sawtelle Boulevard, is just ten minutes from my house and has been a cherished institution in Los Angeles since 1956. I freely admit that I have patronized this fine baking establishment on numerous occasions in the spirit of supporting local enterprise, of course.

The story goes that Ralph Primo and his wife were driving along Sawtelle one afternoon when their three-year-old son saw a sign with a giant donut on a building and shouted, "Donuts, donuts!"

Just like Marisol did yesterday.

Ralph pulled over, went in to buy a tasty treat for his boy, and in the process inquired about part-time work. He was going to school at night and needed something to help make ends meet.

When he returned to the car with a dozen glazed, he told his wife, Celia, that not only had he bought the donuts, he'd bought the shop as well. Sixty-two years later they are still going strong. They'd had their annual pre-Halloween costume party this past Saturday for the kids in the community but were still making these spooky-themed donuts fresh for another few weeks.

Attribute it to my twisted wit, but I was dying to see Augie and Inspector Mason chomp down on spiderweb donuts and skeleton éclairs.

As I was getting dressed, this was a "casual but I mean business jeans and dress boots" kind of day, I rehearsed in my mind how I wanted this meeting to go. First and foremost was to get everyone in the mood to share. Fried dough tends to do that to people. I was prepared to spring for two dozen if necessary.

Jack was in charge of getting Mark to Primo's, and since this had been Marisol's idea, I had no choice but to have her tell Augie about the meeting. The duty of inviting Inspector Mason fell on me, and thankfully he accepted—probably for the lack of information I gave him. I asked Peggy to come along as she, by association, represented another branch of law enforcement. Plus when I asked her, she told me that her guys had turned up some interesting news about the guys that own Provident Commerce Group. She gave me a hint and asked me not to say anything until she had confirmation. I drove, and Marisol and Peggy played "rock, paper, scissors" for who got to ride shotgun.

* * *

Even before we got out of the car in the parking lot behind the shop, sweet, baked goodness wafted out through the air-conditioning vents. The aroma really did make everything rotten in the world disappear for a moment.

The inside of the shop is pretty simple, about one third is used for the customers and the lion's share in the back is for baking, which is done all day on the spot. Three-tiered glass cases display the huge selection of sweet treats, and a banner on the wall behind it shows off the many awards and accolades that Primo's Donuts has received for over six decades. I'd called ahead and requested a dozen be ready on a tray for us.

We gathered around one of the few tables in the shop and waited for our coffee orders (or tea in my case) before starting. Augie and Inspector Mason eyed each other, wondering what they were both doing at this meeting. I was treating them to the donuts, and I warned Marisol that if she ate more than two, I would be escorting her to the car.

When we were all amply supplied with sugar and caffeine I began.

"Thanks, everyone, for coming. I don't know what procedural boundaries this breaks, but I am most certain that sharing information will help to solve this case in the long run."

I saw Inspector Mason take in some air, gearing up to let me know that I'm a civilian and I need to leave this up to the professionals.

"Before you all tell me to mind my own business, I want to throw it out there that I have information concerning one of the suspects in the strip mall fire that I don't believe any of you are in possession of. So let's play a game of 'quid pro quo,' shall we?"

"If you have anything that could help in the arrest of this arsonist, you are obligated by law to tell the authorities, Halsey."

Augie said this showboating for Mason and Mark, not sure which way they were going to lean.

"I'm happy to share what the DEA has tracked down," Mark said. "In fact yesterday we scored a positive ID on some Oxy that was sold in the Marina."

That got inspector Mason's attention. "Mark, do you have any idea when the opioid sale was made?"

"I'll double-check, but I'm pretty sure that the deal and the bust all went down yesterday." Mark pulled out his cell phone and sent a text.

"Which means that it couldn't have been Rico, Inspector, because you have him in jail," Peggy surmised.

Mason nodded. "Correct, but he could have had a courier make the sale."

"If I might ask, what exactly is it that you have that makes Rico such a certain suspect, Inspector?" I was using my most polite voice. "It appears that the evidence that's been found is awfully circumstantial."

"This is where the 'quid pro quo' comes in," Mason said, biting into a long donut iced to look like a tombstone.

"Fine," I said, watching Mason eat. I must have made him self-conscious because he put down his food. "You know the alibi that Brandon gave everybody about being out surfing that Sunday of the fire?"

Heads nodded.

"He may have been at the beach, but he probably wasn't catching a wave. It seems that the dude can't surf. He's been fished out of the water and resuscitated

by paramedics on at least three occasions that we
know about, and when he does paddle out he is scourge
of the regulars for causing wipeouts. On the day of the
fire, I have a witness that surfs the same beach, and
he said that Brandon had essentially been banned."

I gave them a smug look not because the info was
so great, but because I was holding out with something even better.

"Augie, if you're not going to say anything, then
you don't get a donut," Marisol said, trying to take the
delicacy out of his hand.

"We didn't know per se that Brandon couldn't surf,
but we are accumulating evidence that points to he
and Roberto running cons of a number of varieties at
the beach," Augie said, raising his donut-clad hand
way above Marisol's head.

"Who the hell's Pursay?" she snapped back at him.

"Does the evidence that you have show that they
were dealing in narcotics, Augie?"

Augie shook his head. "No, it was petty stuff like
helping people start their cars. Surveillance cameras
from a bank showed them waiting behind an elderly
man who was withdrawing money from the ATM. The
gentleman then paid them for their "repair" services.
From their faces it looked like they were just having
fun, like this was a joyride or something."

"Damn kids thinking that they are entitled. Good
thing they never tried anything on me," Peggy spoke
up. She'd been keeping to herself at one end of the
table, nibbling on a muffin and working her iPad.

"If Brandon and Roberto had no problems breaking the law, what's to stop them from burning down
the mall to collect the insurance money? You're the
only one that hasn't contributed to this share session,

Inspector Mason." I turned to look at him, and the rest of the table did the same.

"That's a considerable leap from scamming a few bucks to arson, Halsey. Plus our evidence indicates that the person that started the strip mall fire knew what he or she was doing. A sophisticated delay incendiary device was used to allow lots of time for the person that placed it to get far away from the site. For this to happen according to plan, it had to be tested, adjusted, and practiced multiple times."

"Sounds about right to me," Mark said, giving me a sympathetic look. "And unless Brandon is smarter than he looks and acts . . . we'd have caught him by now if he was trying to sell Oxy. You don't just walk along the Venice Boardwalk touting 'opioids for sale.'"

"Thanks, Mark," I said, draining the last of my tea. I looked across the table and caught Marisol taking another donut from the pink box, but I was getting too dejected to do anything about it. I had bigger battles to fight. "Mark, were you able to confirm that the sale and bust your guys did all happened yesterday?"

Mark grabbed his cell from his windbreaker and looked at the screen.

"Yes, after some intensive questioning the guy said that he bought the drugs at around ten in the morning, and we busted him attempting a resale at one sixteen. And I know you're going to ask this next, Halsey. He can't identify the seller. He wasn't given any names and the guy was wearing big dark sunglasses and a hoodie tied tight around his face."

"We're still running leads on the owners of the strip mall," Augie jumped in. "This is a real slippery cover-up, so it's like peeling an onion back or opening a set of those Russian nesting dolls. Every time we think we're getting down to the names of the real owners, another roadblock comes up."

I looked at Peggy and gave her a slight nod.

"We've got something more to throw into the soup," Peggy said, closing the cover to her tablet and leaning closer to the table. "It is going to both surprise you all and enlighten you. But I'm only talking after you spill what you've got, Mason."

Marisol got up, dragged her chair around next to Peggy's, and gave Mason her death stare and gold-toothed scary grin.

Two moms and three toddlers entered the donut shop, forcing us to tightly circle the wagons.

"Rico Bruno has a sister," Mason began.

"So what?" Marisol said a bit too loudly. "I got eight of them."

We glared at her until she relaxed.

"Her name is Aurora and she's married to a guy named Matteo Ricci. They live here part of the year, but their permanent address is on the Italian island of Sardinia. What we have on them, him especially, is very thin at the moment, but this Matteo is thought to have committed insurance fraud on a number of occasions. His large family invests in real estate all over the world. This is way out of my department's league, so we've gotten the CIA involved. None of you can say a word about this to anyone, you understand?"

We acknowledged him, and I mimed a knife slitting a throat to Marisol.

"This is why we have identified Rico and perhaps his relatives as our prime arson targets," Mason concluded. "So, Halsey, what do you and your friend Peggy have to add to this?"

"Again this goes no further," Peggy started. "I was a field service asset for the CIA after the Korean war ended, working with the Santa Monica Airport." She lets that settle with everyone before continuing. Marisol started petting Peggy's sleeve, and I brushed her hand away. "It was a close-knit group back then. We all lived and worked in the Mar Vista neighborhood, had barbecues, babysat each other's kids, and such. Some of those kids grew up and went into the family business, so to speak. That's about as deep as I'm prepared to divulge. Anyway, from time to time, I might ask someone for a bit of news if the information is laying around."

Peggy flipped open the cover of her tablet.

"This investment company Provident Commerce Group does not own the burned-down mall property nor any others in the Los Angeles area. They are a management service for shell corporations that retain ownership of the real estate."

Augie got his flip-up leather notepad out of his suit coat pocket and began taking notes. At that same moment one of the toddlers escaped his mother and wandered over to our table. He seemed to be fascinated with Marisol's face. She gave him a smile, leaned in, and whispered to him, "This lady is going to give you ten bucks to go back to your momma. Do you want ten bucks?"

Marisol turned to me and motioned with her pointy chin to the kid. I found two fives in my purse and passed it over. The kid disappeared faster than wood at a termite convention.

"You're acting like you have more information to impart, Peggy." Mark retrieved a pitcher of ice water from the side counter and filled a paper cup for her.

"I do, and this part saddens me terribly, given what Inspector Mason has just told us. My sources were able to track down paperwork identifying the actual company that has the deed to the strip mall. It is called Cagliari Mattoni e Malta. Cagliari is the capital of Sardinia and the other two words translate to 'bricks and mortar.'"

"*Brava*, Peggy." I gave her a soft applause, but she didn't look happy.

"I sense that a shoe is about to drop," Mark said, watching Peggy.

"One of the principals in the company is a man named Matteo Ricci." Peggy looked down almost in shame.

"Wow," said Mason. "So you and my department have been working two ends of the same stick. I don't have time to deal with this now, but I promise to circle back the moment that I'm able. I don't imagine that too many people know about your access to privileged intel at the CIA."

Inspector Mason briskly left the shop about the same time that both Mark and Augie got calls. Not long after they were gone too.

"If no one else's going to eat this last donut . . ." Marisol reached in for the kill.

Chapter Twenty-two

When I was a kid living on the East Coast, we called the night before Halloween Mischief Night. I would latch on to a group of older kids and watch them pull pranks like sticking a pin in a doorbell to make it ring constantly. Tossing rolls of toilet paper up and over tall pine trees was another favorite most often performed by the junior varsity football team. One year the guys took a VW Bug that was parked in a driveway and carried it over to the neighbor's driveway.

Still one of my all-time favorites.

In California they don't really have a name for Halloween Eve, and on Rose Avenue when the sun goes down the activities on the street are not unlike any other evening: grills are lit, dogs are taken on their post-prandial walks, and kids negotiate with parents for "ten more minutes" of playtime outside.

So I was surprised when Penelope called that morning to suggest that we come out and stay the night as well as the night of Halloween and the harvest.

"Some of our neighbors tell us that tonight is really something to experience out here in the hills of

Malibu," she informed me. "There are bonfires, hay rides, and all sorts of those quaint things you Yanks do."

"Wow, Penelope. As you remember here, it's just another night in paradise."

"I know. When Malcolm found out about all the events, he said that it would be a shame for his in-town friends to miss it. Since you lot were all planning on driving up in the morning, do you think that you could push it forward and be here in time for supper? It will be simple . . . we'll just do burgers and bangers on the grill."

It took me a moment to remember that the Brits call sausages "bangers."

"Sounds like a blast, Penelope. I'm going to convene an emergency Wine Club over the phone, and we'll work out the logistics. I'll give you a call once we're on the road."

"Lovely, Halsey. See you soon!"

I am so excited! We all need this: two days of youthful exuberance and two nights of puerile friskiness. Hello!

Sally needed to move around doctors' appointments, Aimee was going to negotiate shift changes with her staff at the yogurt shop, and Peggy sped off to the nearest camping emporium to pick up the supplies that she insisted we needed to work outside after dark.

The only one who was packed and ready to go was Marisol. And I found her that way when I knocked on her door to see if she could leave today instead of tomorrow morning.

"Want me to put these in your car?" she asked,

motioning to two small suitcases and a suit bag with hangers sticking out of the top.

"What's all this? You don't change clothes that much in a year to need all this luggage," I said, wondering now if we needed to take two cars.

"We're going to be there for Halloween, and I need all the pieces for my costume. I guess you're going as a wino, so all you'll need is a bottle and a big glass."

"I resent that, Marisol."

"You resemble it too."

"Do not."

"Do."

I could have let this continue until one of us slugged the other, but I needed to talk to Jack about corralling the men.

"The plan is to leave at four this afternoon and you're only allowed one bag." I left her to pare down her travel clothes and returned home.

"Hello, my beautiful bride," Jack said, picking up my call.

"Hello back, to my handsome dog-training, wilderness-rescuing, beard-trimming, seafood-loving, and nude beach–going man."

He gave out a hearty laugh. "But we've never been to a nude beach, Halsey."

"Day ain't over yet, pardner." I felt the early onset of frisky coming on.

I filled Jack in on the change of plans and explained that Sally's husband Joe would prefer to leave tomorrow as he had afternoon classes to teach today. Wednesday was also better for Tom as he was waiting for the results of some lab work and needed time to go over it.

"I know that you are jammed today, Jack, so could you drive the guys up to the winery tomorrow? You'll need to swing by the Santa Monica Airport too. I told Peggy to have Charlie text his fight schedule and estimated arrival time."

"Sounds good, honey. Don't get into too much trouble tonight; the farther north you go on PCH the closer you get to the ghosts of the Chumash demons."

"The what?"

"You haven't heard about this, Halsey? Do I finally get to scare you?"

"No, you're not scaring me . . . yet. Just give me the four-one-one about this myth."

"The Chumash tribe of Native Americans lived along the coast of Southern California some tens of thousands of years ago, Halsey. I know you love the history of California, so look them up. Anyhow, they believe that the demons are supernaturals of the lower world that show themselves to humans and can cause great joy and great pain. They are prevalent up around Santa Barbara County, and this is their favorite time of year."

While Jack was yammering on, I'd moved into my bedroom and surveyed my closet for something that I could MacGyver into a scary costume. *Damn you, Marisol.*

"Okay, Jack, so what do I do if I encounter one of these demons? Is there a secret prayer that I need to utter? Should I take my invisibility cloak?"

"Very funny, Halsey. I take it that you've never seen *Buffy the Vampire Slayer*?"

"What? Now you're just messing with me, and I've

got to get ready to leave. Love you, and I'll see you tomorrow."

I ended the call and pulled down the little overnight suitcase that I keep on the top shelf of my closet. I still didn't have an inspiration for a costume.

I wonder what Buffy would do?

I'd cleared out any unnecessary baggage from my trunk and neatly placed my one duffel bag smack up against one side.

"What the heck is that, Marisol?"

We were loading up the car, and with five of us plus Bardot, it was going to be a super tight fit. I decided to let Jack bring the wine corker gift, which was fine since it was still in his truck.

"You said that I was only allowed one suitcase, Halsey." Marisol had dragged this thing all the way across my lawn, leaving a strip of flattened grass in its path.

"That's not a suitcase, that's a steamer trunk. The kind someone brings on the *Titanic* when they plan to make the long and dangerous trip across the Atlantic."

"I'm just doing what you told me," she smirked.

"Don't worry, Halsey, we'll tie it to the roof rack," Sally said, appearing on the scene and trying to calm me down.

"Marisol or the suitcase, either works fine for me."

"Remind me never to travel with you again," Marisol said, sliding into the front passenger seat.

"Oh no you don't, missy. You and your short legs go in the back. Sally is sitting up here."

Marisol gave me an angry look but finally complied.

"Hi, everyone!" Aimee joined the group toting a three-tiered portable cake carrier.

"Oh boy, that looks like precious cargo." Peggy studied the car's space options. "Sally, do you think that you can ride with that between your legs during the drive? That would be the safest bet."

I cringed and waited for her response.

"Peggy dear, it would be my pleasure."

Whew, did we just dodge a bullet?

"This isn't the sweetest thing that I've had between my legs, but it's a close second!"

And she went there.

"Aimee, what about Isabella? Did she already drive up?"

"Yes, Halsey. She went early this morning with all her prep and supplies for the pizza. She is just distraught that Rico won't be able to be by her side."

"And Rico still refuses to say where he got the advance for the pizza oven, huh?"

"Unfortunately, yes, Peggy."

His clamming up made the thought that Rico was working with his sister's husband seem plausible. Which means that he could be working with a crime family. True or not he's making it very difficult for us to help him.

"Okay, have we got everyone on board?" I asked, sliding into the driver's seat.

"Aren't you forgetting someone, Halsey?" Marisol grinned at me.

I looked around, stumped.

"Bardot!" they all screamed.

Crap.

I ran back into the house, got her, and locked up

again. I had a feeling that I was going to need my number two in command more than ever on this adventure.

Peggy had hopped back out and was reloading the luggage in the very back of my SUV to make a spot for Bardot. It was either that or go with the idea of putting Marisol on the roof and have Bardot be the third in the backseat.

When we were once again all situated, I turned to Marisol.

"Thanks. I would have been a very unhappy camper if I'd forgotten my best friend."

Marisol grinned, and for once it wasn't evil.

"We're off. I hope everybody's got everything they'll need, because once we hit PCH I'm not turning back."

"Testicles, spectacles, wallet, and keys," Sally said, touching the corresponding places on her body. "Yep, we're all set."

Chapter Twenty-three

By the time we began ascending the serpentine road to the main house of the winery, it was close to six and the sun had definitely decided to punch out for the day. I was grateful that it had held off long enough for us to arrive, because I wouldn't want to hazard that drive in the dark.

I parked in the same spot that Jack and I had done on our last visit but was prepared to move the car when we found out where we would be staying. As soon as we came to a full stop, my passengers began spilling out of the car anxious to take in the splendor of the winery.

"Welcome to the Abigail Rose Harvest weekend, my lovely friends." Penelope approached us followed by a black ball of fluff that had doubled in size in just a few short weeks.

"Malibu Rose!" I bent down to cuddle her, and Bardot decided to join in the huddle, sending me to the ground, which gave Malibu easy access to lick my face.

"Marisol, come meet Malibu Rose, a giant schnauzer

just like Jack's dog Clarence. She'll grow to be almost that big."

Marisol, showing the only sign that she's still a little tender from her accident, lowered herself gingerly, and Malibu went crazy with excitement.

"I'm keeping her," she announced.

"Perhaps not, dear Marisol. The girl has become quite accustomed to having acres and acres of land to run free."

"Looks like she's grown quite accustomed to you as well, Penelope." Peggy gave her a warm hug.

"I've never been here at night, and this place is just magical." Aimee gazed along the mountaintop with moist, admiring eyes.

As if on cue, warm, amber exterior lights began to illuminate the buildings, pathways, and majestic trees.

"Does someone want to rescue these sweet delights from between my legs so that I can get out too?" we heard Sally plead from inside the car.

"Oops, got it." Aimee ran to the rescue.

Penelope looked at me, not sure what to expect next.

"Aimee has baked some much-anticipated pies, cakes, and other goodies for our stay. We were tight on space, so Sally was chosen to cradle them between her legs for the drive. Don't worry, they are safely sealed in plastic containers." I clarified the situation.

"I wasn't worried one bit, Halsey. Come along, everyone. You'll be staying in the barn, which we only yesterday finished work on. Malcolm is beside himself with pride about this achievement, and I must say that I am too." Penelope giggled and led us the short distance to a long, rectangular structure made of stone and concrete with a tin, high-pitched roof.

Peggy hooked my arm and whispered, "It's been a long time since I've laid down in a hay loft."

"I don't think that it will be that rustic. Do you?"

"We're about to find out."

Sally was the first one through the heavy oak-paneled door that Penelope had pulled open with some effort.

"Bless my soul and bring on the mariachis!" Sally followed that with a series of squeals and "oh mys."

"Something tells me that we're going to be okay, Peggy."

Aimee and Marisol caught up, and the five of us stood staring in awe into the barn, acting as if the doors to Oz had just opened.

"This is breathtaking," Aimee whispered as if she were in church.

"It sure is," Peggy also whispered.

"I'm going to claim my room," Marisol said in full voice, pushing past us.

We stepped into an enormous space, larger than the deceptive perception that you got from looking at the exterior. First and foremost, your eye went straight back to a floor-to-ceiling river-rock fireplace with a chimney that must measure over thirty feet tall. There was a lovely fire roaring, and Sally had taken up residence in one of the soft leather club chairs placed in a horseshoe shape around the hearth. There was a matching buttery brown sofa that looked to be able to accommodate six comfortably. On either end Pendleton blankets were draped over the back in case the fire wasn't quite enough for a super cold night.

In the middle of this area sat a round wrought iron and wood table large enough to lay out a seven-thousand-piece jigsaw puzzle.

We joined Sally by the fire.

"Where's Penelope?" I asked, sinking into the sofa and noticing the ceiling for the first time.

"In here, luv. I'll be right over with a tray of goodies and some wine. Aimee, since you're closest, would you mind grabbing some glasses off the rack?"

I saw that Penelope was standing behind a bar arranging a tray of cheeses for us. The light was on in the room behind the bar, which I guessed was a small kitchen. My eyes went back up to the spectacular ceiling. Exposed beams gave the space a rustic warmth and also served as platforms for iron chandeliers to suspend. I wasn't sure where to look next, there was so much to take in.

On either side of the fireplace, wooden shelves were set into the stone wall and filled edge to edge with books.

Wine, books, a roaring fire? Just don't forget to call me for supper.

I followed the bookcases to their tops, and that's when I saw that there was a balcony that went all around the four walls of the building. It looked like it jutted out about twenty feet, and that's when I surmised that the bedrooms had been built up there. It was confirmed when Marisol peered over the railing curiously concurrent with Penelope placing a tray of delectables on the coffee table.

"Right then, my darlings, let me give you a proper welcome," Penelope raised her glass to us.

"This is the most wonderful, beautiful space I've ever seen, Penelope. I feel like I'm in a Ralph Lauren commercial," Aimee gushed.

"I agree, and I wish I'd packed my sleeveless mauve polo shirt." Sally shook her head.

"Why don't you ever get this kind of cheese?" Marisol asked me, stuffing a laden cracker in her mouth.

I ignored her and turned my attention to the echoing sounds of clicking toenails approaching from behind us.

"There they are!" Peggy clapped her hands as she watched exuberant Bardot and euphoric little Malibu Rose come pounding up to us.

I don't think that I'd ever seen Bardot happier. Except maybe for the first time that she discovered that she could dive underwater.

"I thought that I heard the rumblings of a Wine Club in here."

I turned to see Malcolm stride into the barn. All this manual labor was giving him muscles too. No wonder Penelope never stopped smiling. We all cooed accolades on him for this beautiful barn. At his side was Isabella.

"Isabella!" Sally got up to greet her with a hug. We all joined in—we're group hug kinds of folk.

"Hi, Malcolm." Peggy broke off and gave him a hug too.

"Hello, ladies, and welcome. Penelope, Andrew, and I are so happy and proud to share our first harvest with such dear friends." To Penelope he said, "The guys are working the fire in the clay oven, and it should be ready for food in no more than ten minutes."

"Perfect. I'd better get to the main kitchen then." Penelope set into action.

"I'll go with you to help," Isabella said, "and I'm excited to test out the new pizza oven." The second that she said it, her face dropped as I expected that she was thinking of Rico sitting in a jail cell.

"We girls should bring in the luggage and select

our rooms. I have a feeling that later tonight we may not know which end is up." Sally ushered Aimee and Peggy out to the car.

"Marisol, I think that you'll find two bowls and a tin of dog food in the kitchen behind the bar. Would you like to give these two crazy pups their dinner?" Malcolm asked.

"Sure," she said, but made sure to grab the few remaining pieces of cheese left on the tray.

"Halsey, let's sit for a moment . . . there's something that I want to talk to you about."

This was the most serious look I'd seen on Malcolm's face since they returned from their honeymoon. Anguished might be a better way to describe it.

"You're scaring me, Malcolm. What's wrong?"

"I've been keeping something a secret, and it's tearing me apart. I hate like crazy to betray a confidence, but if I don't people will suffer. You've always had such a wise mind, so would it be okay if I share this just with you?"

Are you kidding? Secrets are my bread and butter. As long as they don't hurt the people that I love.

"This sounds ominous. I think you'd better . . . at the very least I'll be able to share the burden."

"Whew, thanks, Halsey." He moved onto the couch next to me so he could speak softly and still be heard.

"It's about Rico."

"Oh God, you have evidence, don't you?"

"Yes, but not for what you think."

I could have sworn that I saw a dark shadow dart across a section of balcony above us.

"As everyone's said, the man is tremendously proud. Foolishly so if you ask me." Malcolm's cheeks were turning candy apple red probably from both the fire and the unburdening of the truth.

"I agree, and I keep wondering if this is just to protect his name or if he's protecting family members that have committed a crime. Or crimes."

"I'm pretty sure that it is the former." Malcolm looked up at the balcony as well. At least I wasn't dreaming that there was movement up there.

"I wish that I could be so sure," I said. "But Inspector Mason and his team seem to have enough evidence. I heard from Augie that he'll be going to the DA with it early next week."

"Then I have to break my promise to Rico, and maybe you can tell me what to do with this."

"Go ahead. What is it, Malcolm?"

"I gave Rico the money to purchase the pizza oven."

"You did?"

"Well, he insisted that it be called a loan that he plans to pay back as soon as the insurance money is paid. Of course I would never accept a payback. After all, the oven is a necessary piece of equipment for our tasting room and private events. We'll get much good use out of it, and besides, the Brunos will need the insurance to rebuild their shop in Mar Vista."

My mind was racing, and I could feel myself hyperventilating.

"Malcolm, do you have proof of this loan, a canceled check, perhaps?"

He dropped his head and shook it.

"I'm afraid not. The condition of the loan was that it be untraceable because he didn't want Isabella to find out that he had needed to borrow money. Like I said, foolish pride."

"So what? You handed him ten thousand dollars in cash? In a briefcase or something?"

Malcolm chuckled. "You watch too many cop movies, Halsey."

I shrugged.

"No, I gave him a cashier's check made out to 'Cash.' He said that he was going to make the purchase directly through an outlet that deals in slightly used equipment."

"Think, Malcolm. Were you here when the oven was delivered?"

"No, I was meeting with a distributor in town. I think that Andrew signed for it."

"Who has the paperwork now? If we can show a paper trail back to you to corroborate your claim that the money came from you, then they'll have to let Rico go!"

"I can check in the office, Halsey."

"MALCOLM? What are all these women doing here tonight? Hell, you told me that they weren't coming until tomorrow."

The shouting came from Andrew standing at the entrance of the barn.

"How the f- am I supposed to get my work done with these busybody bitches wandering around?"

It was then that he saw me sitting with Malcolm. His jaw dropped and he immediately spun around and stormed off.

"Wow, I've never heard Andrew speak that way. What was that all about?"

"Don't take it personally, Halsey. This is Andrew's first big job, and the stress is getting to him."

Or are those his true colors?

We both stood.

"I see. Let me talk to the girls, and we'll make sure to stay out of his way."

"Wonderful. Thanks, Halsey. And right after dinner, I'll go in the office and search for that receipt for the oven."

"Great. Let me know if you want another set of eyes to look with you."

Malcolm nodded.

"I smell beef being grilled, so let's get some chow," he said, walking me toward the doors of the barn.

"I'm just going to run upstairs for a second and freshen up, and I'll be right behind you," I told Malcolm.

I think the thing that struck me as the strangest about Andrew's outburst was not so much that he revealed his temper but that it was directed at the Wine Club "busybodies" interfering with his work. It was now almost seven thirty, pitch-black outside. Just exactly what kind of work was he planning on doing tonight?

When I reached the patio off the side of the main house with the newly built clay and stone oven the mood was decidedly more upbeat.

Penelope was working the grill, flipping burgers and rolling "bangers" over until they were a golden brown. Buns were toasting away from the flame, and a platter was awaiting the finished product. Malcolm took the tongs away from Penelope so that she could be relieved of cooking duties and enjoy her guests.

Behind them a long picnic table with a plastic checkered cloth held buckets every two seats with utensils and napkins in them. About the same distance apart I spotted condiments, bowls of potato salad, pickles, and small bags of chips. And, never one to forget, bottles of wine.

Strings of lights with paper lantern shades were strung across the entire space above us and a fire pit had been lit. I guessed that this was where we'd rendezvous for late-night Calvados and ghost stories.

This is casual and perfect.

To everyone except myself, because I was finding it hard to shake Andrew's acerbic tantrum.

"There you are, BFF!" Sally slid over on the bench to make room for me.

Across the table Peggy and Marisol were having an animated conversation, but with the music and Penelope and Malcolm's staff laughing and talking loudly, I couldn't make out what they were saying. I was certainly going to follow up with Peggy when I had the chance.

I looked to the other side of Marisol and felt my blood boil.

Sitting on the bench almost shoulder to shoulder were Bardot and Malibu Rose, each enjoying plates of cut-up hot dogs that were placed on the table. Jack would have plucked his entire beard out if he'd seen this.

Much as I wanted to put a stop to dogs eating off the table, I really didn't want to ruin the comfortable vibe that was sweeping the group.

Malcolm appeared at the table with a heaping platter of freshly grilled goodies, and from the other side of the table Aimee and Penelope came from the kitchen bringing deep wooden bowls of marvelously delicious-looking salads. I spotted orange wedges of clementine and slivers of almonds, heirloom tomatoes, and multicolored lettuce leaves. And croutons. I tried to catch Aimee's eye so that I could direct her to deposit her bowl in front of me.

"I wonder where Isabella is," Sally leaned in and said to me.

Looking around I deduced that one other person besides Isabella was missing. Andrew.

I was about to get up to look for them when I heard a fork clink on the side of a wineglass.

"If we could have everyone's attention for just one minute," Malcolm began, "tonight we will be enjoying the wine made from the previous harvest before we took ownership of Abigail Rose Winery."

"And in about fourteen months we'll be decanting the claret made from the grapes that we'll be harvesting starting tomorrow." Penelope held her glass up high.

"So let's toast the vines, God's good earth, and warm sun, and the water that gives them life." Malcolm raised his glass as well, and we followed suit.

"To the Abigail Rose Winery!" Andrew shouted as he walked up next to them. He didn't have a glass in hand but did a slow clap instead.

Kind of eerie.

"To the Abigail Rose Winery," everyone replied, and drank.

I watched Malcolm pour Andrew some wine and offer him a seat at the table.

"Don't fill up until you've had some pizza." Isabella appeared with two round sheet pans filled with slices. "There are two more if you want to grab them, Aimee."

Applause broke out again, but this time it was uproarious.

I grabbed a glass and filled it for Isabella.

"Come sit next to me, Isabella. I feel like I haven't

seen you in ages." I patted the bench and she stepped over and released her weight onto the seat. She let out a breath.

Her face was flushed, which should be normal for someone that had just pulled pies out of a hot oven, but this red was all over her face, not just on the apples of her cheeks. Penelope's kitchen was much more open and airy compared to the cramped space at her old pizza parlor, and I'd never seen her this sanguine.

"Cheers, Isabella." Sally leaned in with her glass as well.

"Thank you, sweet friends."

We spent the next few minutes savoring our food.

"This pizza is just as good if not better than I remember you making. I take it that the new oven is working out well?" Sally asked.

Cue the waterworks.

Isabella both nodded and began crying.

"Will you excuse me? I want to see if they'll let me talk to Rico one more time before he goes to sleep."

"Sure, honey. I'll come find you in a little bit. Maybe we can have some wine together by the fire pit," I offered.

"That would be nice, Halsey."

"I hope that I didn't set that off when I asked about the oven, but she looked like she'd been crying when she first walked in." Sally shook her head.

"Of course not, Sally, and I noticed that her face was awfully red too. Poor thing. I just hope that we can sort this all out soon and get Rico off the suspect list."

When I looked across the table again, I saw that Penelope had replaced Marisol, and she and Peggy laughed like one had just told the other a dirty joke.

Penelope caught my eye and rose again to address the table.

"Okay, loves. Please allow me to tell you about our upcoming activities both tonight and tomorrow. Malcolm and Andrew have left to start the bonfire in the open part of the field on tier one. We've set out Tiki torches to guide the way, and it is a short walk down the main road. The fire won't be in full bravado for about an hour, so plan on starting down at about a quarter to ten. In the meantime, enjoy more wine, and Aimee is going to lavish us with some sumptuous sweets."

Applause erupted and wine bottles were passed. I should have just sat back and let the fun of the moment sweep me away, but I couldn't help but let my thoughts drift back to the fire and its suspects.

"Now, as for tomorrow," Penelope continued, "we've got several trucks of day laborers that will be arriving at half past five in the morning. They will be starting their picking at the lowest tier and then work their way up the hill. You're on your own for breakfast, but the barn kitchen is filled with anything your heart could desire, and I plan on delivering fresh fruit and breads around six. Don't fuss about getting up with the dawn. I expect this will be a late night and we won't be ready to harvest the first tier before noon. That is where we'll set you lot up to help with the harvest."

I wonder where Bardot has gone?

"One last thing: the night before Halloween is meant to be the scary one around this area, and lore has it that native American demons roam the grounds looking to morally corrupt the humans they encounter."

"Oh dear, Peggy, have you got anything left that

hasn't been morally corrupted?" Sally asked her, and laughed.

Some of the others were laughing but not all. Aimee's eyes were so wide you could sit teacups on them. I peered under the table, hoping to catch my dog working on a burger. *No such luck.*

"I'm told that this is all in good fun and that the scary beings we might encounter are most likely friends from the next winery over—welcoming us with a little Chumash myth fun. But if something feels really off, don't take it lightly. I've encountered some things since I've lived here that I find difficult to describe in any other way but 'supernatural.'"

If she was trying to scare us, Penelope had succeeded.

"I'm going to find Bardot," I told Sally.

"Look for Marisol and I doubt that Bardot will be far behind. Especially after that feast of table food she served her."

"Good point, Sally, and it will be the perfect time to murder Marisol because everyone will assume it was the demons."

I extracted myself from the table and stretched my limbs. It was time to track down Bardot and then find Malcolm. It was imperative that we search his office for proof of delivery of the oven and its distributor.

No one had gotten around to putting out the torches yet, so I made my way down to the road by the light of the moon. I'd left my cell phone in my room to charge before heading off to dinner.

The road was dirt and gravel, and if you couldn't watch your steps it was very easy to slip and slide. Which is exactly what I did, landing on my forearm and elbow. I could feel the road claiming a layer of my epidermis.

"Ouch!"

I got myself upright again and proceeded more gingerly. I started to hear male voices and figured that I was getting close to the path onto tier one.

"How could you, Malcolm? You broke the code of honor among men, and we never did that on my side of the family!"

"Don't be so melodramatic, Andrew. If I didn't speak up, I'd essentially be turning Isabella into a widow. You know that they're never going to let Rico out of prison."

"Because he's guilty! Who else could it be? I know what it's like to slave away all day for little pay. Unlike you. Great-Grandma Rose was ripe for the picking when you found her, wasn't she, Malcolm?"

I was getting close and I didn't want to run the risk of being spotted, so I edged over to some thick bougainvillea to hide behind. I crouched down so that I could find a "peep hole" in the branches to observe them. All of a sudden I felt something wet on my injured arm.

"Ack!"

"Ssh, Halsey, they'll hear you," a voice whispered next to me.

I turned to see Marisol sitting cross-legged with Bardot beside her. Bardot resumed licking my arm, and then her tail wagging made loud rustling noises against the branches of the bougainvillea bush.

"What are you doing here?" I asked Marisol softly.

"Same as you, listening to these two yell at each other."

I stilled Bardot's tail and put my index finger to my

lips. She understood the signal and got into a down position. I leaned over to look through the natural clearing that Marisol had found.

"Andrew, you know very well that I had nothing to do with Abigail Rose's death. We've been all through this."

I could see both men using pitchforks to pile up branches, leaves, and debris. With each bit of arguing their movements got more determined.

"You also chose to do nothing about sharing the inheritance with a last remaining blood relative, didn't you, Malcolm?"

"I didn't even know that you were alive and in this country at the time, Andrew. The first time that I saw you in person since childhood was when you drove up to the winery about a year ago. And I didn't know that we were blood relatives until a few months after that when you took a saliva sample to send off for a DNA test!"

What? Andrew had said that it was Malcolm who had found him.

"I told you things only someone who had been a kid with you would remember."

"And I took you on and gave you a job and room and board, Andrew."

"Oops, I forgot to throw you a party. My name should be on the deed for this vineyard along with yours, Malcolm. Not your interloping wife that you've only known for sixteen months or so."

At that Malcolm dropped his pitchfork and opened up a can of gasoline. He started pouring heavy douses on the pyre.

"Stop that. You're going to drown the fire before it even starts. Don't you know anything about combustion?"

Andrew tried to grab the can away from Malcolm and they ended up wrestling to the ground. Andrew outweighed Malcolm by at least fifty pounds, so the battle was soon over. But in the process I'd seen gasoline spill out onto Malcolm's clothing.

Andrew stood over him, the can in one hand and a book of matches that he'd pulled out of his pocket in the other.

I gave out an audible gasp.

Andrew turned in our direction and froze.

We did the same.

In the next moment a large owl took flight, and from behind Andrew and Malcolm I could hear voices and see light being emitted from torches.

"That's got to be some of the guys from Bergsteen Winery," Malcolm said, getting up.

The voices got louder, and I nodded to Marisol that it was time to go.

Chapter Twenty-four

"Where's Malibu Rose?" I asked Marisol when we'd reached the top of the hill and the main house.

"She's sleeping in your bed. Poor little thing was pooped."

"What? Why my bed? And I'm not surprised that the puppy was tired after all that toxic food you fed her."

"You ate it too and you didn't die. And she's going to want to sleep next to Bardot later, so I saved the puppy the trouble of moving."

"There is so much wrong with that logic. But we'll get back to this. Right now we need to round up the girls and tell them what we witnessed."

"Just open a bottle of wine and they'll come swarming."

"Very funny . . . let's get to the barn."

As we passed the main house I had an idea.

"You go on ahead, Marisol. There's something that Malcolm asked me to look for in his office. I'll be along in a few minutes. And don't feed Bardot any more food!"

"Okay, okay, meanie."

I crept up onto the patio and entered the house through the kitchen doors. I was hoping not to be seen, but if I got caught I'd just say that I was looking for Penelope. The room was dark except for some lights on the pizza oven and over the farmhouse sink. A wrought iron rack was suspended from the ceiling above the island counter in the center of the kitchen. Utensils and pots and pans hung down on hooks all around the rack. In this light they looked more like goblins, hovering and waiting to attack.

Stop it, Halsey, you're scaring yourself!

I'd barely spent any time inside the main house, so I had no clue where Malcolm's office was located. There were three ways in and out of the kitchen: the one to the patio and two doors on opposite walls of the space. It was a toss-up, so I went with the one to my left. The door opened into the next room, which was pitch-black. I reached into my pocket for my cell phone.

Rats.

I remembered that it was charging in my room in the barn. I was going to have to feel my way along the walls, because I wanted to avoid switching on a light until I was in the office. I had offered to help Malcolm search for the receipt for the oven, not go in on my own and snoop around. Who knows how long he and Andrew would continue arguing at the bonfire, and now that they had company from another winery, they could be there all night drinking and bragging and telling stories.

I knew that for each day that Rico was in jail, Inspector Mason was strengthening his case. And now, thanks to his temper, Andrew had cast himself into the spotlight as a viable suspect.

I heard footsteps nearby and froze. The moonlight had helped my eyes adjust a bit to the dark, and while I could make out little more than shadows, I was pretty certain that I was looking at a person moving about at the far end of this room. I flattened myself as close as possible against the wall behind me, and on my back I felt an uneven surface that I couldn't immediately place.

There were intermittent banging noises coming from the back of the room, and I suspected that the person groping around did not want to be identified either.

The noises were getting closer.

All of a sudden I heard a thud, the rumbling sound of something moving, and a muffled groan. I felt the wall at my back vibrate with increasing velocity, and the rumbling got closer.

Then I felt the swish of cold air breeze past my face, and I made a loud intake of air. The other person in the room must have heard me because next I felt the vibration of footsteps breaking into a run. A sliver of light showed and extinguished itself quickly as the door to the kitchen was open and shut.

I was hyperventilating and still frightened by what had just whipped by me.

I waited a few moments but heard no other sounds. When I dared, I turned around to face the uneven wall and tried to figure out what made it that way. Parts of the wall had a little bit of give, moving slightly forward and back. The wall was made not of stone or even of wood, although parts felt like timber.

I was finally able to work one of the pieces loose and it fell to the floor with a thump. I kneeled and felt around for it, and when I found it I realized that it was a book.

I must be in the library and that thing that swooshed by me, and scared the other person off, was probably a ladder!

I slowly calmed my breathing. I wanted to follow whoever had been in here with me, but I knew that this could be my only chance to find the proof that I needed in Malcolm's office. Even though the cashier's check could be traced back to the bank he withdrew if from, there was nothing to tie it to Rico unless I found a receipt for delivery.

I opened the door at the back of the room a crack and peered through. It led to a big atrium, and I guessed that this was the foyer of the main entrance to the house. I listened and when I was satisfied that I was alone, I crossed the floor to another door, which was already ajar. There was a light on somewhere in the room. I knocked lightly just in case there was someone in there. I decided that it would play better than sneaking in.

When I didn't hear a response, I entered the room.

Bingo! This must be Malcolm's office. There was a desk in the center of the room, and one wall held shelves of curios that I recognized from his great-grandmother Abigail's collection. There was the old La Union cigar box that had set off the whole mystery surrounding her death. There was his family's collection of antique carnival and amusement park memorabilia, from when they had worked at the Venice Beach attractions after the turn of the twentieth century. Some family members had been legit, and some were bona fide con artists. And in a glass and wooden case in the corner of the room was an antique tommy submachine gun with its classic magazine drum. The history of how it came to be in the family's possession is vague but its more recent use is not. A couple of years ago Malcolm's great-grandmother, who had lived on Rose Avenue, went missing. She'd been at a very advanced age and was in the final stages of Alzheimer's disease. As the fickle finger of fate had latched on to me, her body turned up buried in a garden plot—my garden plot—in the community gardens on the hill east of Rose Avenue. It was Bardot's helping me turn the soil to plant grapevines that cleared the soil to reveal her old, bony hand. I'll spare you all the details, but I can't look at that gun without remembering that it almost killed me when we discovered the culprit.

I shifted my attention to Malcolm's desk and re-alized that it had been thoroughly searched and ransacked. By, I'm guessing, the mystery person that passed me in the library. They had to be looking for that receipt. I couldn't think of another reason for this mess.

Who stands to gain the most if Rico takes the fall for the fire? Up until now I wouldn't have thought Andrew, but he was becoming a more and more likely suspect. If the evidence had been found or not, there was no point in me going over what had clearly been an exhaustive search job.

No longer worried about being spotted, I exited the house via the main door, but I jumped back in almost immediately to avoid being run over by an El Camino lowrider half-bed truck traveling way too fast toward the dark roadway out of the winery. Introduced by

Chevy in the early sixties, these half truck, half cars of glistening chrome, bright colors, and mirrors spawned a culture in California for big cars cruising low and slow. Catch a Cheech & Chong movie if you're still not picturing it.

The car slowed and kicked up dirt to be able to take the turn for the road down the hill. When I craned my neck out again, I saw Bardot leap into the back of the truck. When she saw me—and then didn't—she must have thought that I'd hopped in for a ride.

Marisol caught up with me huffing and puffing.

"Sorry . . . one minute, Bardie was right beside me. The next, she was gone."

"Not your fault, Marisol."

We both watched helplessly as the truck went through the first turn of the winding dirt road.

"Huh."

"What huh? Do you recognize that truck, Marisol?"

"Maybe."

"Is it the one that tried to run you over?"

"Could be but they really weren't aiming for me, just going fast."

I got one last glimpse of the back of the truck and could see Bardot looking back at me confused. As the vehicle braked for a switchback the license plate was briefly illuminated. It read, CRKNEE. I bolted for my car.

"Where are you going?"

"Bardot's in there. I've got to save her!"

"Then I'm coming too."

Marisol picked up speed and actually beat me to the car.

I hope that I'm that spry at half her age.

"Hey, sister, where're you going?" Sally asked as I backed out of the parking area.

I rolled down my window.

"Bardot jumped into the flatbed of a truck thinking that I was riding in it. Someone is speeding down the road with her, and I've got to catch up or I might never see Bardot again."

"Oh Lordy, Lord. I'll find Penelope and Malcolm and we'll catch up to you with flashlights. Drive carefully!"

"What the hell's going on? I lay down for a short nap and everything is going to hell in a hand basket," Peggy declared, joining Sally from the barn.

"I'll fill you in on the way, but right now we've got to find Penelope!" Sally grabbed Peggy by her fleece vest and pulled her toward the main house.

I took the first turn a little too fast and we skidded sideways on the gravel. I let off the brakes so as not to send us into a full spin. When it was safe, I applied some gas and pointed us down the hill again.

"Marisol, did you see that license plate? Does it ring a bell from before?"

"No, what'd it say?"

"It was a personalized one, just the letters C-R-K-N-E-E."

"Nope, but I only saw it from the front. After I fell on my knee I didn't see anything for a few minutes."

"Say that again, Marisol."

"What? The whole thing? Why?"

"No just the last bit."

"After I fell on my knee . . . this is stupid!"

My heart was racing and once again we started to slide off the roadway. This time I hit the gas and straightened us out.

"Don't you get it, Marisol? Say the spelling of the license plate out loud."

"I already forgot it."

"Fine, then I will. The first two letters are CR which could be short for 'CAR.' And the second group of letters spell 'KNEE.' Put them together and you have something that sounds like 'CARNEY.'"

"Great, what do you want? A marching band with trained monkeys?"

"Don't you get it, Marisol? That has to be Andrew in that truck trying to get away. He comes from a family of carnival scam artists."

"So does Malcolm."

"True, but what reason would he have to be running away? Surely you don't think that Malcolm had anything to do with the fire?"

"I dunno. Watch out, HALSEY!" Marisol screamed, and ahead all I saw were blinding headlights speeding toward us.

I reached across the front seat to hold Marisol in place and took a sharp turn to my right.

And that was when everything went to black.

I tried to open my eyes, but the second that I let any light in my whole head pounded in anger.

I was breathing so I guessed that I was alive, but I had no clue where I was or how I'd gotten here. I felt the space at either side of my body and concluded that I was lying on my back and that beneath me was dirt.

Maybe they're digging a hole and getting ready to bury me!

"Halsey?"

I faintly heard a voice utter my name.

"Babe, are you okay? We gave you a quick check and nothing appeared to be broken, but tell me where it hurts."

I kept my eyes shut, but I was beginning to get my faculties back. The voice sounded like Jack's. I felt warm air on my cheek and then a kiss with tongue on my lips.

Really, Jack?

Then the warm breath shifted to my ear and again the tongue went in for the kill.

I sure as hell hope that we're alone, Jack.

When I then heard a series of sniffs and leaves rustling, I realized that they were caused by a tail wagging and that the sloppy kisser was in fact Bardot.

"What happened?" I tried to sit up and was unsuccessful.

"Honey, don't try to move just yet." This time I knew that it was Jack speaking.

And then I remembered.

"Marisol!" I sat up abruptly. "Is she okay?" I opened my eyes to try and see for myself.

"She's much tougher than you, Halsey," I heard another voice say, and looked up for its owner. Staring down at me, I could make out Augie and Marisol.

"You're both a sight for sore eyes. Hi, Bardot. How did you get off the truck, my sweet girl?"

"We passed it on our way up. It had come to a stop, and I saw something jump out the back and run into the fields."

"Rico?" I asked, wondering if I was hallucinating.

"Correct. They let me go, Halsey."

"How about we first get you on your feet and back up to the winery so we can properly check on your injuries, hon? I think that it would be best if we call the paramedics." Jack put his arm under my knees and hoisted me up to his chest.

"No! Seriously, I really am fine. Just ask Sally to come up and take a look at me," I pleaded.

He set me down in the backseat of his truck and Marisol joined me. Bardot also wouldn't leave my side.

"Be right back. I think Augie, Rico, and I can get your car out of the ditch and back on the road," Jack told me.

"I feel pretty stupid driving off the road because I thought that some 'demon' was trying to kill us."

"Usually I'd say you are stupid, Halsey . . . and drunk. But not this time."

"I appreciate the vote of confidence, Marisol."

We heard wheels turning in gravel, and I ultimately saw my poor car pull out onto the road. There was visible damage to the body over my front wheel, but I couldn't count on that being the only problem until I took it to a mechanic.

"Okay," Jack said once his head appeared through the backseat window. "It actually sounded pretty good when we started her up. Augie and Rico are going to drive it back to the winery, and then we can put some lights on it and take a closer look."

I watched my poor, dusty car head up to the winery. Both Augie and Rico had the windows down, which was just going to let in more dirt. I'll need to get it detailed for sure.

Jack got behind the wheel and turned on his

truck's massive headlights and side searchlights. The road lit up, revealing all its twists and turns.

Maybe I need searchlights.

I could see Jack looking at me in the rearview mirror. "Augie called me a couple of hours ago to find out where Isabella was. He said that Inspector Mason had been sent a text with a receipt attached showing delivery of a pizza oven to the winery. Mason was able to contact the distributor and confirm that they had been paid with a cashier's check, drawn from Malcolm's bank."

"Thank goodness. Malcolm must have found the receipt sometime this evening and sent the text." My brain was slowly starting to charge its pistons.

"I don't think that it was Malcolm, but Augie will know." Jack was safely and easily driving up the hill when we encountered Penelope leading Sally, Peggy, and Aimee down the road with torches. Jack rolled down his window.

"Jack, you made it tonight. I guess you couldn't bear to be without your sweetheart for even one night," Penelope teased.

"It's a little more complicated than that. Halsey and Marisol had an accident and drove off the road."

"What?" Sally screamed.

"She seems alert and Marisol is fine," Jack said, trying to calm her down. "Let's meet up at the winery where you can examine her more closely."

"Take her directly to the barn," Penelope instructed. "We'll meet you there. Sally, I have a most impressive first aid kit that you can use."

"What about Bardot? Did you find her?" Peggy was also getting frantic.

"She's on her back snoring on the seat right now, showing us her coochie in all its glory," Marisol hollered from the backseat.

"That girl, she's something," Aimee said, smile/crying.

"When you arrive, bring Halsey to the sofa in front of the fire, Jack."

"Will do, Penelope."

Chapter Twenty-five

Jack drove the rest of the way up and pulled over into the parking area that we were all using.

"Slide over a bit, Halsey, and I'll carry you into the barn," Jack offered.

"I want to try my legs out and see how I feel. Can you just help me up?"

"Sure, babe."

I stood and was grateful that I didn't feel any shooting pain either up or down my legs or my spine. The only place that was throbbing a little was my backside.

"I'm starting to remember what happened. I think after the car stopped, I had this premonition of it catching fire and having trouble getting out. I must have released my seat belt, opened my door, and rolled out. For a moment I guess I forgot that I drive an SUV and landed directly on my backside."

"You did and all the while you were yelling 'I didn't start the fire,'" Marisol explained, extending her hand to help me walk.

Billy Joel? Really? Was he to be my last dying thought?

Augie and Rico arrived and parked beside us.

"Rico, I have no idea where Isabella is, but Penelope is meeting us in the barn and I'm sure she'll know."

"Thank you, Halsey. Let me help you walk." Rico took my other arm, and the two pretty much acted as human crutches.

Once we were settled on the sofa and club chairs, Jack knelt beside me and checked for damage.

"Does this hurt?" He touched my knee and I shook my head. "How about this?" he asked, checking both my wrists. Once again, I shook my head.

"Jack, there is only one spot on my body that must have taken the brunt of the impact when I fell out of the car."

"It has to be her bootie, she landed right on it."
Thanks, Marisol.

Jack was about to roll me over when I stopped him.

"Sally will be here any second. Augie, did you call Inspector Mason or did he call you?" I asked, sitting up and then feeling the weight shoot straight to my butt.

"He called me," Augie responded, looking concerned for my injuries. I remembered that he was very squeamish when it came to medical conditions and especially needles. I'd hoped that there was one in Penelope's first aid kit. I'd hardly had any fun this evening.

"Here we are," Penelope said, riding in on a golf cart. Her passengers were Sally, Peggy, and Aimee. Even Bardot woke up, sensing a party brewing.

"I'm going to take your vitals first," nurse Sally explained, relieving Jack.

"Augie, where'd you come from?" Peggy looked bewildered, wide-eyed. When she saw Rico, she went into full-on confusion.

Augie recounted the story of the receipt, the text to Inspector Mason, and Rico's resulting acquittal.

"If you don't mind, Miss Penelope, I'd like to see my wife. Do you know where Isabella is right now?" Rico pleaded softly.

"She wasn't down at the bonfire. What happened, Penelope?" Malcolm asked after entering the barn and seeing Sally taking my blood pressure.

"Hello, darling. I'm so glad that you're here . . . Halsey and Marisol were in an accident on our horribly dark road to the vineyards. We need to get lights installed immediately."

"The electrician's coming on Saturday, my dear," Malcolm assured her. "Is Halsey going to be okay?" He peered over Sally's shoulder at me.

"Her vitals are stable, and she's confided in me where her pain is centered. I'm going to need to examine her privately," Sally stated matter-of-factly.

"She busted her butt," Marisol translated.

"Then let's get Halsey up to her room." Penelope took charge. "If you boys want to wash up and get something to eat or drink, Malcolm can show you to the downstairs bath and kitchen."

I really didn't want to move . . . the warm fire was so comforting, the buttery soft leather sofa was cradling me in its arms, and the people and dog that I love surrounded me. When I didn't move right away, I started to get concerned looks. I didn't want to have the ambulance discussion again, so I got to my feet.

Penelope smiled and swung an arm over my shoulders. "Rico, follow us, and I'll show you where Isabella is staying. Poor dear, she's probably fast asleep after such a busy evening. But everyone agreed, her pizzas were absolutely divine."

"Great, so the clay oven in the patio worked well, yes?" Rico asked.

"What? Oh no, luv, she baked them in the new oven. That definitely made a huge difference."

Rico stopped in his tracks. "Oh, did someone light the oven for her?"

"I don't think so." Penelope looked to Malcolm and he shook his head. At this point we were all stopped on the second-floor balcony.

"She doesn't know anything about the oven heat-up procedure, so she wouldn't know how to light the pilot. She always said that she was afraid of the fire." I saw fear in Rico's eyes.

"Augie?" I shouted down to him.

"Yes?" He looked up at me.

"Did Inspector Mason tell you who sent him the text with the receipt attached?"

"I believe that he said it was Andrew, why?"

"Penelope, which room is Isabella's?" I asked.

It was the second one in. Penelope tapped at the door and then tried the knob. It opened, and she switched on the light.

"It's empty . . . she's not here!"

A flood of images and words suddenly were placed in the correct order in my mind.

"Quick," I shouted. "We've got to get to the grape-vines. I have a strong feeling that incendiary devices are being set around them as we speak."

"Why?" Malcolm shouted back to me.

"Because I think that someone wants your entire harvest to go up in flames!"

* * *

We followed Malcolm to a separate structure that served as a storeroom/garage. He doled out high-power flashlights and two-way radios that we made sure were all set to the same channel. I saw Marisol's eyes light up at the introduction of equipment used in espionage.

There were also three more golf carts charged and ready to go. Jack took charge, my manly man.

"Malcolm you take a cart, and, Peggy and Sally, you go ahead and ride with him."

They nodded and took their seats.

"Augie, you take this one and Rico and Marisol."

"Got it," he said.

"We need to cover as much ground as possible because the fire starters could be set anywhere. In this dry brush a fire will spread quickly," I informed them.

"Exactly, so, Aimee, you ride with Penelope and I'll take Halsey and Bardot," Jack concluded. "Malcolm, do you want to assign each of us a tier?"

"Right. We'll double up on the lowest tier because it has the most acreage." Malcolm continued his instructions as he passed out fire extinguishers for each party.

"Are you sure about this?" Jack whispered to me when we got into the cart.

"Pretty much. I just don't know one hundred percent who will be holding the match."

"There's only one way to find out." Jack backed the cart out and we headed down the hill toward the second tier.

"Tell me how your thinking got you to this point,

Halsey?" Despite the urgency, Jack was taking the curves slowly. One crash a night was enough.

"The first big hurdle was deciding if the fire and the stealing of the drugstore safe were two separate crimes or one big act of defiance. I kept going back and forth on that."

"Understandable."

"Then with the attrition of suspects and my gut belief that Rico would never commit a crime, let alone arson, the field slimmed down quickly."

"This looks like the entrance," Jack said, and pulled off onto a narrower pathway that ran the side of the hill in between rows of grapevines. He stopped the cart and we surveyed the scene. Below we could see intermittent lights from the first-tier search teams.

"I guess we should just go along one row to the end and then switchback to the next?" Jack tugged at his beard.

Clouds that had formed as a result of the temperature shift to colder air had obscured the moon. We were riding low, and I was struck by how dry the ground was as compared to say, strawberry fields. I remembered overhearing Andrew tell Sally earlier at dinner that grapes are a dry climate fruit. If you restrict their water the right amount during the season they'll work harder to grow and become their most flavorful. He certainly knew his viticulture, which made it difficult for me to imagine his wanting to destroy these beautiful vines.

The pathway between the rows was dirt with sparse bits of grass growing thanks to stray spritzes of water that came off the irrigation system. The vines themselves grew out of short root stocks and were supported by a trellis made up of several rows of heavy wire attached to posts about six feet high.

Bardot's eyes were wide open, and her nose was working overtime. Noticing this, Jack said, "I think that we need to put Bardot to work."

"This might help." I produced the piece of orange plastic from my pocket and let her take in a good, long sniff.

"What's that?" Jack took it from my hands for a closer look.

"It's something that was found in the ashes after the fire."

"You mean like evidence? How did you get this? Shouldn't it be with the police or fire inspectors?"

This line of questioning was going to land me in hot water with Jack, and we had bigger fish to fry just now.

"I'll explain later, Jack. I'm going to send Bardot loose and we can follow slowly behind. Use your flashlight along the base of the vines. You're looking for mounds of brush with maybe a wine bottle underneath."

"Okay, but I'm not forgetting about this."

"Of course you're not."

"How long do you guess it will take these timed devices to ignite, Halsey?"

"From the little bit of research that I've done, I say ten minutes, max. I need to radio everyone and tell them what to look for."

I kept my eyes on Bardot while I relayed the information. When I was done, I had a thought and got back on the radio.

"Hey, Rico? This is Halsey again."

"Yes?"

"Odd question, but what do you usually use to

ignite the pilot light in your pizza oven?" I was reaching, but the right response would tell me a lot.

"I have a box of these sticks that are made of wood and paraffin wax."

"Hey, Halsey?" This time it was Malcolm speaking.

"Hi, Malcolm."

"We use the same sticks to light the clay oven. There's a big box of them in the kitchen if you need any."

"No, Malcolm, I don't, but I suggest you look out for them on any piles of brush that you find."

"Will do. Oh no . . . there are flames right in front of us. Got to go!"

Just then Bardot stuck her nose in the air and then took off like a shot down the path.

"Follow her!" I told Jack.

"I'm trying, but Bardot is way faster than this bucket of bolts."

It was hard to keep up and see her. Jack accelerated the cart and it bumped and jostled us, making my hand holding the flashlight go haywire. The vines with their lush leaves spread wide along the row, making it easy for someone to hide among them.

I tried to keep a light on her even though she was far ahead of us. If my butt hadn't been so sore, I would have gotten out and ran. I watched as she came to a stop, stuck her head into the leaves of some vines, and wagged her tail. I hoped that last gesture was a good sign.

When we caught up with Bardot, I shone my flashlight around the area. I recognized her yellow tail swishing among the grape leaves. Then the light caught a pair of hands wielding an orange forked tool on the other side of the vine.

"I barely caught this one in time," said a male voice. "Had to sacrifice some grapes I'm afraid."

"Andrew?" I asked. Jack was out of the cart in a flash and moved into position between the two of us.

I put my hand on Jack's arm and tugged him gently back beside me.

"How did you know what to look for, Andrew?"

"I heard it on the radio; you all have been blabbering for over an hour."

I nodded, letting that piece of the puzzle sink in.

"What is that orange thing that you're holding?" I was transfixed on it.

"This?" Andrew opened his hand to reveal that it had an orange forked end about four inches long attached to a black corrugated handle. "It's a grape razor harvesting tool. Penelope insisted on orange for the winery, in honor of Malcolm's hair I guess."

"So, you didn't have anything to do with the fire in the strip mall?" Jack asked, stunned at the realization.

"Hell no, is that what you think, Jack?"

Andrew stood up with grapes in one hand and a waxy stick in the other.

"It's a good thing that the damp sea air blew in or these things would have gone up like Chinese lanterns. I can finish this row if you want to hit the top one. I suspect that the culprit is long gone by now."

"Bardot! Come on up." I patted the backseat of the cart.

"This might be a rude question, but why does she like you so much?" I sheepishly said to Andrew.

"It could be these." He pulled a baggie out of his pocket. "Dried mangoes. I got hooked on them when a fellow surfer offered me one after we'd paddled out. Great source of antioxidants and gives you an energy boost between sets. Bardot sniffed them out when we met at the block party, and I must confess I've been sneaking them to her ever since. I did check that they are safe for dogs to eat." Andrew grinned and shrugged his shoulders. He was back to being cute again in my eyes.

I watched Andrew lope off along the row of vineyards to search for more incendiary devices. Bardot looked at me and I could tell that she wanted to follow him.

"It looks like there's a fire starting on the row above us, so we'd better boogie, honey." Jack started up the golf cart and we headed up.

"See you at the top," Andrew shouted back to us.

"I'm totally confused," Jack said once we rounded the switchback and drove toward the flames. "What just happened back there? And, more importantly, who is setting these fires?" Jack's raised voice showed his frustration.

"You're about to see. I'm afraid that my intuition was correct," I said as we came to a stop. I doused the fire with one of the extinguishers.

"You might as well come out, Isabella," I said, clearing some leaves out of the way.

Jack shone his flashlight into the vines and caught Isabella's face. She was smoking a cigarette. I flashed back to Isabella admitting that when Rico wasn't looking, she'd occasionally sneak out for a smoke with Brandon and Roberto.

"Where's your partner in crime, Isabella?" I took her hand and pulled her to her feet.

"I don't know what you are talking about? I am

trying to put out the fires just like the others." She couldn't look me in the eye.

"Augie? We're going to need you on tier two," Jack said into the radio.

"Go ahead, Isabella, call out his name," I challenged her. "No reason to protect him now and the truth is going to come out."

"Not Rico?" Jack asked me.

I shook my head.

"Go on," I ordered.

"Okay." Isabella took in a breath of resignation. "Brandon?"

"Yeah?"

From the top row of this tier we heard the rustle of leaves and the crunch of dry earth. We shone our lights in that direction and caught Brandon coming down the hill toward us. He still looked like an aimless surfer dude in board shorts and a graphic tee, but his facial expression betrayed a sense of worry going on inside. When he got close, we lowered our lights so that he could see where he was walking.

"Oh shit," he said, recognizing Augie in the group. "Are we busted?" he asked Isabella.

"You are," Isabella replied quickly. "I was here trying to stop you. Ungrateful snot that you are."

That was an entirely new tone of voice I was hearing from Isabella, and it served to confirm my suspicions.

Augie put Brandon in zip tie restraints and sat him down in his golf cart. For added good measure he also secured those restraints to the side rail of the seat.

Once there was no longer a risk of Brandon running away, Augie turned his attention back to us.

"Now, Mrs. Bruno," he began.

"Isabella, please." She gave him a warm smile.

"Right, Isabella. Can you explain how Brandon came to be here among the grapevines? He wasn't invited to the harvest celebration, was he?"

"Not at all, and this is the first time I'm seeing him here," I explained to Augie.

"You'll have to ask him that question, Augie. I had overheard Halsey shout that someone was trying to burn down the fields, and I rushed out to help. It would break my heart if anything happened to this beautiful winery." Isabella started to weep.

"That's a crock," Brandon shouted from the cart.

"If I may," I said to Augie. "Isabella, where were you when you heard me express concern about a fire?"

I'd said it on the interior balcony of the barn, just after we discovered that Isabella wasn't in her room.

"Where was I? Where you all were, of course!"

"So you were in the library? I didn't see you there." I was laying out a trap that should work unless someone else says something to ruin it.

Isabella nodded. "I was there but standing on the other side of that rolling ladder; maybe that hid me from view. I didn't realize."

"Jack and Augie, have either of you been in the library in the main house?" I pushed on.

"You mean the bookshelves on either side of the big fireplace in the barn?" Jack asked.

"No, this is an entire room in the main house. With a floor-to-ceiling library ladder on wheels, just as Isabella described."

"Then no."

Augie shook his head as well. "We've only been

here for maybe two hours, so we've only seen the barn and that garage where we got the carts."

"You must have been with the others in the library or maybe it was another room. I've been up and working for about twenty-two hours, I'm very tired." Isabella looked from one of us to the other to show her sincerity.

"Of course, Isabella, I understand. And once again the pizza was spectacular. You'll have to try some, Jack. If there are any leftovers that is. How on earth did you light that brand-new pizza oven? It didn't look like something you just put a match to or flip a switch."

"No, you don't, Halsey. It is quite a process and not something that you want to do if you're timid around fire." Isabella made herself stand taller, proud of her accomplishment.

"So, you did this all on your own? Rico said that you were always afraid of even going near the oven." I was closing in.

Isabella realized her mistake and quickly tried to backtrack.

"Me? I watched from a distance; it was Andrew who got it going."

"I did not!" Andrew had climbed up from a lower row to join us. "You seemed to know all about those ovens, Isabella, remember? You assured me that you could have it up and running at least a day before the harvest."

"I never said that, Andrew."

"Of course you did. It was on the patio the day before everyone arrived. It was just after you asked me if I had the receipt for the delivery of the oven."

"So, Isabella was trying to clear Rico despite his foolish pride?" Jack asked.

"Not exactly, more like the opposite. She was trying to destroy the evidence that proved that Malcolm had paid for the oven." Just as I finished saying that, Isabella took off in a sprint. She didn't get far. Andrew's strong surfer legs caught her almost immediately.

Augie zip-tied Isabella's hands and led her to our golf cart.

"I suggest that we pick this up on level ground now. I'll let Malcolm know what has happened, and when they are satisfied that all the incendiary devices have been destroyed, they can join us.

Andrew sat next to Isabella in the backseat to make sure that she stayed put on the ride back up the hill. Bardot and I climbed into the front next to Jack.

"Have I ever told you that you're brilliant?" he asked me.

"Not nearly often enough."

Chapter Twenty-six

We gathered in the kitchen because all this excite-ment had given everyone a ravenous appetite and thirst. Augie had called for a couple of squad cars to take the suspects to jail and wanted to run through the sequence of events and clues with us before the police arrived.

If you ask me, I think that he was beyond pleased that he had made an arrest in at least part of this case.

The big kitchen island was resplendent with cold burgers, salads, cheeses, pizza, and desserts. Some were eating right from the platters—too hungry to fix plates.

Once Augie had staved off his need for nourish-ment, he began.

"Okay, everyone, forgive me in advance if I seem to be overly meticulous about the details that I am going to ask you about, but I must be thorough. You two will be asked for your statements when we get you to the station," Augie said, looking at Brandon and Isabella, stiff-cuffed and seated in wooden chairs.

"Thank God everyone is safe!" Aimee screamed, running into the kitchen and hugging each of us. I doubt that she even noticed that Isabella and Brandon were restrained.

"I hear that you've solved another mystery." Peggy patted my back and winked.

"Not without everyone's help and wise advice," I replied, hugging Sally who had come in toting a most beautiful looking bunch of grapes.

Malcolm and Penelope came up to me, and we must have stood in a group hug for over two minutes.

"How will we ever repay you for saving our harvest, Halsey?" Penelope asked.

"If everyone would have a seat, please. I was about to go over the events that have led up to the arrests that we have just made," Augie instructed.

"Isabella!" Rico cried, seeing her.

"It's all a mistake, my love, I'll be fine. Brandon is the criminal here."

"You'll be fine in jail for the rest of your life, Isabella." Brandon glared at her. "Roberto was my friend!"

"Quiet! Or I will remove you both from the room, which would deprive you of the chance to tell the truth and perhaps get you a lighter sentence."

I thought that Augie would have removed them anyway. This seemed to be out of protocol, but I guess that he had his reasons.

"We're going to work backward," Augie announced. "I'll sketch out the events and I want you all to add details. "There were two teams looking for fire starters on the lowest tier, Malcolm, Peggy, and Sally—also Rico, Marisol, and myself."

I looked around for Marisol and didn't see her. My bet was that she was snooping while everyone else was otherwise occupied.

"Jack and Halsey, you covered the middle tier," Augie continued.

"Along with me," Andrew chimed in. "I'd heard all the chatter over the radio, saw two carts heading down to the bottom, and decided to start on the middle."

"That was you in the El Camino zipping down the hill, wasn't it?" I asked Andrew.

"Guilty as charged. Oops . . . maybe not the best choice of words. I'd left Malcolm and his buddies from the next winery to tend to the bonfire and walked back up here for a rest and some fresh air. We'd had it out a bit, and I needed to be alone and calm down. There were so many people milling about that I hopped in my truck and decided to head down to the ocean for a bit."

"Did you know that Bardot had hopped into the back of your El Camino?" I asked Andrew.

"Really? No way, I was still a little pissed, and I was blasting music. Geez, she's okay though?" He knelt down to pet Bardot and check her over for injuries.

"She's fine. Did you stop somewhere along the way down?"

"Yes, Halsey, that's the thing. I never made it to the ocean. I spotted a couple of people walking along the lowest tier and wondered if some of the ladies from your group had gotten lost. I quickly veered off the road and went after them."

"Did you catch up to them, Andrew?" Augie picked up the trail.

"No, and I hadn't brought my flashlight from the truck or my radio. I went back to get them and then took up their trail again. About that time, I saw a truck driving up the hill. I remember wondering if the two were related."

Jack had finished his third slice of pizza and was carefully cleaning his beard with a paper towel.

"That would have been us," Jack explained. "I had Rico and Augie with me. Right after he was released, Rico wanted to see Isabella as soon as possible."

Rico groaned loudly.

"I invited Augie to tag along and promised to take him to my favorite fish taco place for a late supper on the way back. I knew that I had to pick up all the guys in the morning, Halsey."

I smiled at my man. Behind him Isabella sat, expressionless.

"Please continue, Andrew."

"I kept searching for the people I'd seen but wasn't having much luck. I'd heard leaves rustling, some whispered conversations that I couldn't quite make out, even footsteps when I thought I was getting close to someone. I kept thinking that it had to be one or two of the girls from Rose Avenue . . . I even called out a couple of your names. After a while I moved up to the second tier. When I saw flashlights and heard carts driving down the hill I switched on my radio. As soon as I heard the news, I started finding fire starters and dismantling them. I was by myself until Bardot and then Halsey and Jack found me."

"Are you really going to go through every minute of this evening, Detective? In another hour it will be light out," Isabella said.

I saw Sally give a slight nod in agreement. I moved over to Augie and whispered, "She's got a point. We'd all be happy to take this up again tomorrow."

Augie cupped his hand to his mouth and said in a faint voice, "I really don't have enough to arrest them,

Halsey, unless we can catch them in more lies. The library question was a good start."

He continued whispering to me for a bit more.

I nodded and stepped back so that Augie could continue.

"Brandon, when did you get here and why?"

Brandon looked at Isabella and paused but then said, "What the hell, she's going to try and throw me under the bus anyway. Isabella called me this afternoon and said that she needed my help tonight with something that was very important."

"And you agreed to help her? That's awfully civilized of you, Brandon. So you two kept in touch after the fire?" I asked him, and he squirmed in his chair.

In the distance we could hear sirens. Augie quickly grabbed his cell phone, punched a number, and said, "This is a Code two, do you read? Shut off those sirens."

Moments later the sound disappeared.

"I kinda had to do whatever Isabella asked, Halsey. You see we were sort of blackmailing each other."

"Sweet Jesus, Mary, and Joseph and pass the marmalade," Sally hollered.

"This boy is clearly on drugs," Isabella said.

"Nope, not unless he just started doing them today. I've had my resources check out Brandon Dawson. His father is an addict, comes and goes all the time," Peggy piped up. "But that must have made the kid not go near them. He's been picked up by EMTs numerous times getting banged up when trying to surf. Each time he was tested, and the results were negative. I just got this news a couple of hours ago, when I checked my emails, Halsey."

Way to go, Peggy!

"Tell us about the blackmail, Brandon," I gently urged him.

"The day after the fire I ran into Isabella when I'd returned to the mall to see if there was anything incriminating that I'd left behind. I think Rico was talking with the insurance guy or something. Isabella said that she knew that I stole the safe from the drugstore and that she'd keep quiet about it under the right conditions."

"Liar!"

"Isabella, don't say anything more," Rico implored her.

"I was scared to death and I couldn't think straight. I told her that I'd do whatever she wanted. That was the day that I met you at the site, Halsey. I wanted to do a quick check to make sure that I hadn't left anything that could pin me in the drugstore. When I heard Inspector Mason's voice, I climbed over stuff and bolted out the back."

Jack had slowly and nonchalantly moved over to where Isabella was seated.

"What were Isabella's demands, Brandon?" Augie was keeping the confession going.

Out of the corner of my eye, I thought that I saw a small figure darting about in the dark side of the kitchen. Bardot's head went up as well.

"She insisted that we split the money from the drug sales fifty-fifty. She said that she was sick of the daily drudgery of running a business and dealing with a deadbeat landlord. She wanted to come work here for Penelope."

"What? She never said any such thing to me about this. You?" Penelope asked Malcolm and he shook his head.

"She'd made that pretty clear to me," Andrew said.

"I gave her a tour of the winery a week before you two got back from your honeymoon. She had a couple of glasses of wine and got swept up in the beauty of the place. She even let on that Rico refused to sell the business. Isabella said they still had bills to pay off."

"No!" Rico was on his feet.

"I may have told Brandon how tired I was, but I swear this whole safe thing is a total lie." Isabella's poker face was starting to crack.

"Brandon, you said that this blackmailing went both ways. What did you have on Isabella?" I walked over to him for his answer.

"Roberto was in on this drug thing. In fact, that was how we were going to pull it off. He had the keys to the parlor, and I was going to meet him outside the back door of the drugstore. The plan was for Roberto to climb up into the attic from the restaurant, crawl over to the location of the drugstore, and enter it from the attic. He'd then open the back door, help me with the safe, and retreat back to the pizza place. He'd then lock up and meet up with me after his delivery shift. Only he never showed."

Four uniformed officers appeared at the entry to the kitchen.

"When I heard that you pulled Roberto out of the parlor, I figured that either Rico or Isabella had run into Roberto in the parlor, and he'd been caught red-handed. Probably clocked him good because he certainly didn't recover in time to escape the smoke and flames." Brandon looked spent and I felt sorry for him. He'd made a dumb choice and was now going to pay for it for a long time.

"Augie." Sally took charge. "Was there an autopsy done on Roberto?"

"Yes, but I haven't had a chance to read the report yet."

"Were you able to sell the opioids, Brandon?" I wanted to wrap this up—everyone was fading.

"Are you kidding? In an instant, I'd already paid Isabella her share, about fifteen thou."

"But she wasn't done with you, was she?"

"Obviously not, Halsey, or I wouldn't be here tonight. When she discovered that Rico had been released, she called me and railed over the phone about how much trouble I could be in if I ever said anything."

"Isabella lured Brandon out to the vineyard, not to burn down the vines." Peggy had caught on.

"That's correct, Peggy. She must have given Brandon some lame excuse for why she needed him to help her at the winery tonight."

"Isabella told me that she had a way to frame Andrew for the theft of the safe. I figured that this was my chance to get out from under suspicion and her control." Brandon shook his head, realizing that neither had happened.

"Instead she saw this as the perfect cover to kill Brandon and make it look like he had tried to kill her. And since Isabella had developed a taste for fire starting, burning the vineyard also gave her a chance to stick it to Andrew, who she'd admitted earlier was a smug rich kid." I'd taken the story full circle.

"You won't be able to prove any of it, and since we're not at the station I'll deny everything and lawyer up." This truly was evil Isabella coming to the surface.

"That's okay, Isabella, we have a cooperating witness who will swear to the facts discussed here."

"Who? Brandon? We all know he's a loser, and I sure didn't see anybody taking notes in here." Isabella was getting back some smugness.

"Not notes; I got much better stuff." Marisol walked out of the darkness and into the lighted area of the kitchen. A headset rested on her shoulders and around her neck.

"You got it all, right, Auntie?" Augie asked.

"Every last bit of it." She grinned and saluted Peggy who returned the gesture.

"I didn't agree to this, and you didn't read me my Miranda rights . . . none of this will be admissible in court."

"Of course not, Isabella," Augie replied. "We don't intend to use anything you said on this recording in court."

"But Augie did have a chance to Mirandize Brandon, and he agreed to participate in exchange for consideration at sentencing." I revealed what Augie had whispered to me.

"You two can take Brandon back to the station now," Augie said to the cops. "You did great, son, and I'll make sure to put in my recommendation for leniency. But you've still got to tell us the details of your car repair scam," he said to Brandon.

"Oh, he did great all right." Isabella's face was red and screwed up like an old apple. "You and Roberto were talking so loudly during your robbery that I'm surprised some of the neighbors didn't make a 'disturbing the peace' call. Roberto was so proud of himself that he didn't see me hiding in the attic above our place. He passed right by me on his way back to the restaurant.

After I'd set my timed device and Molotov cocktail—the wine bottle was a tip of the hat to Andrew—I snuck back down and saw Roberto smoking in the doorway. It was easy from there to hit him on the head with a dough hook. I even still had gloves on!" Isabella laughed. "Finding, catching, Brandon in a crime was like having a bag of money land in my lap."

Isabella bolted out of her chair and tried to make a run for it. I watched her locate the door to the library, which confirmed to me that she'd been the one who ransacked Malcolm's office. I stepped in front of her, blocking the way.

"Don't you try and stop me, little miss perfect." Isabella stared at me with wide, manic eyes. "I hated when you'd come into the restaurant to keep me company, the pity oozing out of your pores, Halsey. Things were happening for you, a growing business, a house with a pool, this Wine Club, and the upcoming marriage to a good guy. What did I have for working day in and day out? Nothing!" Isabella spat on the floor. "It's my turn now and I deserve it."

She turned. "You admitted that you can't use anything that I'm saying, Augie, so I might as well have at it. Right? Later tonight I'll demand to see my lawyer, and you'll quickly be told that you have no case. So can't a woman just blow off a little steam?"

Isabella focused her sights on me again and she lunged forward, intending to hit me hard in the chest with her head. Augie grabbed her just in time, and the officers took over with firm grasps.

I looked over to Jack and Bardot. Both were ready to defend me.

Augie nodded to one of the officers.

"Mrs. Bruno," the officer began. "You have the right

to remain silent . . ." He continued until he'd finished reciting her Miranda rights.

"You guys can take Mrs. Bruno to the women's jail," Augie ordered when the officer was done.

"Just one more thing before they take her away, Augie, and this should tie a nice bow around your collar." I was proud of my *Law & Order* lingo.

"Andrew, in the vineyard you were using a grape harvest razor. The blade was held in place by a forked, orange piece of plastic and the handle was made of black, corrugated rubber."

"Yep, as I told you, Penelope had a bunch ordered for the winery. I wonder what the orange signified, Malcolm." Andrew grinned at him.

"When you brought Isabella up here for a tour, did you give her one of those grape razors?" I continued.

"As a matter of fact, I did. She noticed the one on my belt and insisted that she needed one as a souvenir."

"Marisol, you're still recording, correct?"

"What else would I be doing, Halsey? You've kept us up all night."

"In a moment you can hang upside down and go to sleep, Marisol."

"I am taking a sealed baggie out of my pocket," I said . . . for the benefit of the court later. "Inside is a piece of orange plastic about an inch long. There is also a piece of broken-off metal embedded into the forked area. This piece was found among the debris in the attic of the strip mall fire above where the drugstore had stood. Jack, would you like to do the honors with Bardot?"

"Absolutely." He took the evidence bag from me, and Bardot immediately sat at attention. "Bardot is being trained with CARA, the California pet and human rescue partnership that is called into service during emergencies and disasters."

Marisol hopped on a stool next to the island and got to work on the grapes that Sally had purloined.

"Bardot is exceptional at scent tracking, and with just the slightest hint of smell from a lost victim off of a personal item that they've touched, she can follow the scent to the person no matter how far away, over hills and water."

Jack opened the bag to expose the orange piece and let Bardot take a good, long sniff.

"Got it, girl?"

She wagged her tail and hopped up and down on four legs with excitement.

"Track!" Jack said, and Bardot took off. She stopped when she got to the center of the room and lifted her nose to the air. She then ran toward Andrew, sniffed around him a bit, and took in another noseful of air. She then turned and sped over to Isabella, sat, and began her ten-bark sequence.

"Excellent!" Augie said to us, and nodded for the men to take Isabella away.

Rico was sobbing.

"Oh, Rico, you always treated me like I was made of egg shells. I know that's the way you were brought up, but it made me feel useless. I listened when the guy that sold us our first oven went through how to light it. I could have gotten up early and done that each day, but when you wanted to protect me from fire . . . I figured fine, I get more sleep. And more time to learn about fires and arson on the Internet. It is fascinating to me. A fire needs three things to flourish—fuel, heat, and oxygen—and so do I."

"I told you right from the beginning that Bardot's

nose knows. If you'd listened to me then, it would have saved us all a lot of time and I could be having freshly grilled hot dogs with my two best friends." Marisol gave Malibu Rose and Bardot some ear scratches.

I stared at her. Marisol couldn't mean Jack and myself.

"Bardot and Malibu Rose. By the way you might want to change your sheets before you crawl into bed. I might have left the puppy in your room a bit too long. Night, night."

One of these days, Marisol.

Epilogue

I don't know how long we slept, but there was a full sun shining outside when I got up and parted the drapes. Jack groaned and turned over, not quite ready to face the day. Bardot clearly felt the same way and had sneakily crawled into the space on the bed that I had just vacated.

It took a moment for me to recollect last night's events, so I went into the bathroom to wash my face hoping that would make a difference. Malcolm and Penelope had outdone themselves on the barn remodel. The bathrooms were mission style but with modern fixtures and a large walk-in shower that I noticed had numerous spouts.

"I think that we need to test those out," Jack said, entering the bathroom and catching me staring at the faucets and gauges. "The entire family!"

Jack waltzed in naked and unafraid followed by Bardot. He fiddled with some controls and water streamed out and pulsed. He grabbed my arm and pulled me in to join them.

"Jack, I have a T-shirt on!"

"I'll take care of that." He grinned.

* * *

Cleaned and dressed for public appearances, we were ready to venture out to find the others and procure some much-needed caffeine and nourishment. As I opened the door to our room, I noticed a note card had been placed under the door.

"It's from Penelope," I told Jack. "She says that everything that we could want in food and love is waiting for us on the patio of the main house."

As we left the barn the full impact of the day's brightness hit us both with cringe-worthy surprise. We'd been looking forward to the harvest for months, but after last night's ordeal I was afraid that we would be just too worn out to enjoy it. This seemed like much more of a day for eating potato chips in bed and watching movies.

As we were nearing the main house my phone pinged. It was a text from Liza Gilhooly. I opened it and she'd attached a photo of, I assumed, her hand with a big fat engagement ring on it. The text read, *Guess what? Valentin really is my valentine!*

When we reached the patio, I could see a good-size group of people sitting on both sides of the long picnic table.

"There they are." Penelope applauded our arrival. "We'd thought that perhaps you'd wandered down to the wine cellar and were conducting a private tasting."

Upon hearing that, I saw Peggy, Sally, and Aimee look in my direction. If I could read minds, I would say that we were all thinking . . . *Should we? Silly not to!*

"Augie rode back in one of the squad cars last night and Rico drove Isabella's car and followed them to the women's jail," Peggy explained, drinking what looked like a Bloody Mary.

Seeing that, I couldn't think of anything that I wanted more in life.

"I know who tried to run me over with their car behind the mall now," Marisol announced seated next to Malibu Rose, gorging on scrambled eggs and muffins. When Bardot saw them, she was ready to bolt to her place at the table.

"Psst." Jack signaled her, and she stuck by our sides.

"Okay, who was it, Marisol?" I asked, taking a seat and watching Penelope pour me a Bloody. *I am in heaven.*

"It was Isabella. I didn't recognize her driving, but I wouldn't forget her car."

"Why is that?" Jack took a seat next to me and reached for the fruit salad bowl.

"Because it smelled like chicken wings!" Marisol grinned and then went sad.

"Isabella must have been driving the delivery car," I told the group. "Marisol, chin up. I noticed a few days ago that there is a chicken place going in next to Vons. I'll pick some up for you whenever you want."

"She's going to regret saying that," I heard Sally tell Aimee.

"So do you think that this case is wrapped up, Halsey?" Aimee asked.

"The autopsy report should back up Isabella's story that Roberto suffered a blow to the head, so I would say that, yes, Augie has a pretty tight case."

"What I want to know is why? If she was that unhappy and Rico was too proud to admit defeat or ask for help, then why the Sam hill didn't she just take off?" Peggy was showing some anger at the thought.

"It's not that easy for some people," Andrew began.

I hadn't noticed he and Malcolm join us. They must have returned from the harvest because they looked dusty and suntanned.

"I watched my mom struggle and throw in the towel," Andrew continued. "Instead, she chose to try and smoke her troubles away. Several of my foster care moms were in the same boat. My lot in life, until recently, was not much better. A guy out of the foster system with no family and nothing much to show for it doesn't exactly get shown the red carpet when applying for work. But then I realized that I needed to take control of my own destiny, stop letting other people control my fate."

Malcolm squeezed his cousin's shoulder with affection. "Penelope and I have talked about this, and we'd be ecstatic if you would accept our offer of a partnership position at the Abigail Rose Winery."

"Wow, I wasn't expecting this. Hey, man, I'm sorry about the things I said to you last night." Andrew looked humbled and hung his head down with shyness.

"What words? You are family . . . we need to take care of each other." They hugged. "The workers are on the second tier and making great progress," Malcolm told us.

"Hear, hear," Penelope said, joining her men at the end of the table. "And once that's done and the wine is doing its deliciously miraculous thing, then we can move on to the really big event happening at the Abigail Rose Winery."

We all looked at her expectantly.

"The wonderful marriage of Halsey and Jack!"

Cheers and applause erupted. Jack and I shared a look.

Jack gave my cheek a kiss and rose. He wanted to allow plenty of time to soak in the announcement before leaving to retrieve the other men he had agreed to bring to the vineyard later.

"Halsey and I are so super lucky to have you wonderful folks as our close friends. We are blessed, truly blessed."

"Don't tell me there's a 'but' coming. I'll worry the horn off a unicorn." Sally stood and started shaking her hands.

"Don't worry, honey, it's a good thing." I walked behind Sally, sat her down, and gave her a hug.

"We'd better open some wine." Aimee ran into the kitchen.

"You single again, Jack?" Marisol grinned at him.

"No!" I shouted, but quickly collected myself. "What Jack is trying to tell you is that with all the bad things going on with everyone, the fire, health scares, accidents, lies, and betrayals, we didn't want to wait until June to become an official family."

"Oh crap," Marisol said, and went back to eating.

"So we went to the beautiful historic Saint Vincent de Paul Church in the West Adams district of Los Angeles and spoke to a priest about getting ready for marriage. We were lucky enough to secure the twenty-second of December!" Jack walked over to me and held my hand. "And I am the happiest man alive!"

We kissed and didn't stop until we heard the popping sound of champagne corks.

The Rose Avenue Wine Club girls enveloped me in a tight embrace. I saw Bardot take advantage of the moment to flank Marisol on the other side from Malibu Rose.

"Absolutely fabulous," Penelope finally said after the news had registered. "And we can host the reception!"

People were slapping Jack on the back and congratulating him. Penelope had huddled with the girls, and I could hear them discussing party plans.

I spotted Marisol, now by herself.

"Where are the dogs?" I asked, joining her.

"Typical. When the food was gone, they left me to play."

Marisol suddenly looked older—her cheeks had sunk, and her eyes looked sad.

"Are you upset that the wedding has been pushed up, Marisol? Will you need to be home with family? You may invite anyone you wish."

"No." She began to swing her legs on the bench like a little girl.

"Then what is it? You seem kind of down." I gave her a squeeze.

"For a moment there, just for a moment, I thought that Jack was about to reveal his true love."

"He did; you heard him. We're about to get married." I started to wonder if Marisol was actually losing it.

"Yeah, I heard him, and that's when I knew that our love affair was over."

"What are you talking about?!" I shouted.

"Ha, ha. Got you!"

Marisol got up and could barely walk she was laughing so heartily.

I hate you, Marisol . . . okay, I love/hate you.

WHAT THE ROSE AVENUE WINE CLUB DRANK

Tooth and Nail the Possessor, Paso Robles

Helioterra Pinot Blanc, Willamette Valley

Bonny Doon Clos de Gilroy Grenache, Central Coast

Argiolas Costamolino Vermentino, Sardinia, Italy

Heitz Grignolino Rosé, Napa Valley

Lune d'Argent White Bordeaux Blend, Bordeaux, France

Piper Heidsieck Cuvée Brut Champagne, Champagne, France

Coppola Diamond Claret, Napa Valley

Beckmen Vineyards Purisima Mountain Syrah, Los Olivos

GIFTS THE ROSE AVENUE CLUB HAVE OR WOULD LIKE TO RECEIVE

Aerator and pourer: Whether you get them with animal heads, golf-themed, or battery-operated, these nifty devices force air to circulate while you pour, allowing the wine to "breathe." If you have the time and patience (we don't), you can pour the wine into a decanter and wait about an hour. "I'd better be asleep while this is happening," Peggy likes to say.

Bottle holders: Frankly, the Rose Avenue Wine Club's wines aren't around long enough to merit a decorative, fancy display holder. But if someone bestowed upon you a bottle of *Chateau de Rot Gut* for your birthday and you want to make sure it stays out of your drinking rack, here are some options: French waiters, butlers, chefs, a menagerie of animals lying on their backs drinking from a bottle that has been hoisted up by their paws. There are holders in the shape of high heel shoes, baseball players at bat, trains, planes, and automobiles and gravity-defying balancing acts. And then there's Sally's favorite, the twelve days of Christmas wine bottle holder. "I get it all set up and then I don't have to think about what to drink each day!"

Chillers: Didn't have time to properly cool your wine? No worries. There are a plethora of accoutrements to assist you: wine pearls, glacier rocks, wine gems, crystals, chilling wands, and marble buckets.

Corkcicle: Skip the aerator and chiller and have the best of both worlds with a wine chiller and aerator in one! Chill it in the freezer and then pop it into any wine bottle. The pour-through feature aerates while the thermal gel perfectly chills whites and reds. Plus the Wine Club loves saying "corkcicle"!

Decanter: You've all seen them, you may even own one. But how about a personalized duck-shaped decanter? Or a steampunk octopus set? There's one in the shape of a globe that spins on a stand, and you can find those that are bejeweled, bedazzled, and beguiling (the Lalique Aphrodite decanter).

And if you are an enthusiast of a certain subject, ask for a pineapple-, dog-, bull-, guitar-, penguin-, or guitar-shaped bottle.

Purse: Not to be confused with tote bags, these devices are meant to be used for the journey rather than the arrival. A carefully hidden, insulated compartment keeps your wine chilled for hours while to others on the go you look like you are simply sporting a fashionable roomy purse. They even have designer flaps to conceal the spout at the side of the bag. Run into someone you know holding an empty coffee cup? Offer to refresh their drink!

Shower wineglass holder: The Rose Avenue Wine Club always requires a celebratory birthday lunch and often has us combing the marketplace for unique wine-themed gifts. This gem has suction cups to stick to your shower tiles. We suggest drinking something clean and crisp.

Wine balloon stopper: For those rare occasions when you aren't able to finish the entire bottle. Have a plane to catch perhaps? This is basically a balloon, a hose, and a pump. In this case the pump is in the shape of a bunch of grapes. Drop the balloon end into a half-filled bottle and inflate until it covers the inside edges of the bottle. Voilà, you have an airtight place to save your leftover wine. But call the airline before you leave in case your departure may be delayed, in which case you won't need this device.